To
See You

To See You

rachel blaufeld

To See You

Paperback ISBN: 978-0-9970707-3-6

Edited by

Pam Berehulke

www.bulletproofediting.com

Cover design by

© Sarah Hansen, Okay Creations, LLC

www.okaycreations.com

Cover Image

Hrecheniuk Oleksii

Interior design and formatting by

E.M.
TIPPETTS
BOOK DESIGNS

www.emtippetsbookdesigns.com

Warning:

Content contains explicit sexual content and crude language, and is intended for mature audiences. Parental/reader discretion advised.

Dedication

For My Electric Readers –
I wouldn't be here today without you (I don't care if it's a ridiculously cliché thing to say). We're a crazy crew—young and old, American and not, curvy and slender, with long hair and short. But we all love ankle boots and doughnuts, and most importantly, we love one another.
No judgment. Only conversation, support, and a common love of reading.
Thank you for the steady encouragement and daily friendship. You hang, read, share, write reviews, and most of all, believe in my words and me.
We have shared many milestones together, happy occasions and sad.
Here's to many, many more.
This is for you.

And for Nicole –
Who is really my better half, my way better half. The more organized one.
Thank you for decoding my choppy e-mails and sending me reminders and, well . . . just about everything.
Hope to see your smile again—real soon.

About the Book

What is it about this guy?

On paper, he's one hundred percent wrong for me. His e-mails are equal parts annoying and funny.

Okay, more funny than annoying. More like refreshing. Different. Exciting.

But as I stand next to him now, he's giving me head-to-toe tingles, and I find myself dwelling on his e-mails.

Meet smart, sexy career girl and New York snob, Charli Richards. She has everything except happiness until the day she meets Layton Griffin. It's a random encounter on an airplane; it couldn't mean anything, right?

Layton isn't even remotely close to who Charli sees herself hooking up with . . . ever. Her mom and best friend agree he's not for her, but he makes her feel something exciting, awakens her world.

But then Layton changes, going to great lengths for Charli to see him for who he really is.

Will those changes bring them closer together, or will she never be able to see him in the same way again?

Prologue

I half sat, half leaned at the bar waiting for her. It was an overpriced, cliché hole-in-the-wall in Manhattan she'd suggested. *Best burgers in New York,* she'd written in her e-mail. She'd assumed I'd want something big and heavy to eat, overselling the place to me and avoiding the fat fucking elephant in the room.

Which was me, so I didn't take the burger suggestion as a slight. I deserved that one. Especially after the sushi debacle.

But I wasn't one bit hungry for burgers—not tonight. To be honest, I was famished for her. I was so fucking starving for this woman, I'd gone without an apology, showed up like a good little puppy without even as much as an apologetic whisper. No *sorry* or a single freaking misgiving about what had happened the last time we saw each other. Zip.

Now I sat in the bar area like one of those big whales at Sea World, waiting in line for a dead fish. It was dingy and dimly lit, but the Yelpers loved this joint. Of course I'd googled it, making sure I was hip enough to show my face in the establishment.

Impatient, I swirled the Scotch in my tumbler, the ice clinking against the glass. Out of habit, I pulled my shirt down at the waist, making sure it covered my waistband. It was a habit I still couldn't quite shake. I'd worn a waffle-knit shirt and khakis, the new trendy kind, elastic at the ankle and a drawstring at the waist—all the bells and whistles.

I wasn't sure why I felt like I had to forgo my usual look. The only other times we'd met up, I'd been wearing a music tee and jeans. Except for the premiere, but tonight was different from the other times . . . I hoped. That assumption was probably false and premature on my part.

As I took a sip of my drink, the liquid burned the back of my throat and warmed me all the way going down, heightening my arousal and calming my nerves at the same time.

Tiny bells chimed above the door, signaling it was opening—a touch that was out of place for New York City, but I assumed it was part of the charm of this joint.

She stepped over the threshold, shaking the snow off her now longer hair before swiping her gloved hand down the front of her coat. I saw a hint of red peeking out from underneath her black coat, reminding me it was just past Valentine's Day, making me wish I'd come earlier in the month. She could have been *mine*.

She still hadn't seen me, so I indulged in a second or ten, allowing my gaze to roam her small frame all the way down to the fur-lined ankle boots . . . with a heel . . . on her feet.

Unable to get up or move toward her for fear she'd reject me all over again, I turned back toward the bar and caught the score of a basketball game on TV while tossing back the remainder of my Scotch. I felt her presence singe the back of my neck before she laid eyes on me.

Willing myself not to turn and seek her out, I ran a hand through my hair and mentally chastised myself.

You pussy. Just look at the woman.

My hair was styled the same, so she should recognize me from the back. At least, that's the sorry excuse I gave myself . . .

Part 1

One

Charli

Ten Months Earlier

"Oh my God, Mom, do we have to discuss this? Now? Over the phone? Crap."

I bit back a curse as my ankle rolled inside my boot, then stopped and shook out my foot. Stupid me, insisting on wearing stylish wedge ankle boots that were clearly not made for travel. That was me—I hid all my insecurities deep down inside my expensive shoes like a good New Yorker.

"Charli," my mom said with exasperation, the *i* at the end coming out like a very long *eee* as she begged me to listen to her.

"Yes, I know," I said quickly into the phone. "I take birth control seriously. I will . . . I promise to call the doctor. Yes, I swear, but honestly, Mom, it's not important right now. I barely date, and no, Garrett isn't the solution. Listen, I have to go."

For the second time, I stopped in my tracks and looked up at the gate number, checking to make sure I was at the correct one, and only half listened to my mom's reply.

She whined something more about Garrett and him being the solution, and then dropped the guilt card on me again.

"Honey, you need an important man, one who puts on a suit like your dad always did. That's what he wanted for you, and I need you to do that for me. He made me promise you would find happiness."

Happiness. I snorted to myself. *Whatever that is.*

"It's been a hard week, Mom, but I think you're getting overly stressed or something. You're not acting like yourself."

"No, it's not that . . ."

I tilted my head to pin the phone against my shoulder, feeling a jagged pain shoot down my neck and shoulder blade, and I didn't bother to listen to the rest of what she was saying.

"I'm at the gate. I have to go. Don't stress," I whispered, handing the gate attendant my ticket while holding the phone awkwardly, my heavy bag cutting off the circulation in my shoulder.

"You just made it," the woman said with more pep than a cheerleader at the Super Bowl.

"Thank God. I have to get out of here and back to New York, where reality is reality," I told the overly perky blond attendant and shoved my phone in my tote, hoisted it back on my shoulder, and began walking the plank.

My life was a supersized episode of *Bridget Jones.* Except I wasn't chunky and definitely wasn't as nice as she was in that movie. I thrived on the grimy, rushed mess known as the Big Apple. My faltering ego and stunted soul relied on being better than at least half of the other 8.5 million souls in the city. That way, I continued to feel okay with my deficiencies.

As usual, I was the last to board the flight. Eternally grateful for first-class upgrades and checked luggage, I walked through the door and looked toward seat 2C.

Another perky blond airline employee stood in the entryway to greet me. "Welcome aboard."

I couldn't respond because I'd just caught a glimpse of seat 2D. In it was a pretty large man, huge by Manhattan standards, and not in that alpha-male, football-player type way. No, he was big—just big—with half his thigh rolling over into my seat.

Blech. I'd grown less and less tolerant of others during my years in the city. I used to be different, but now I was a cookie-cutter model of two-thirds of the arrogant women in New York. On the small island, I'd grown accustomed to everyone looking like Sarah Jessica Parker or Mr. Big. They were the golden standard of life and love, even though they were fictional and an unrealistic ideal.

There the man was, next to my well-deserved cushy leather seat, the one freaking perk I actually liked about my job. The big career—the one I wasn't sure I even wanted anymore—but at least I could sit in my first-class seat thanks to the frequent-flyer miles I had accrued.

I quickly scanned the remainder of the first-class cabin and saw every seat was taken. His dark brown eyes took in my frown and defeated sigh before they quickly cast down to his open tray. I made a half-feeble attempt to plaster a fake smile on my face and slid into my seat, cocking my whole body toward the armrest nearest the aisle. Without a word, I shoved my bag under the seat in front of me just as they closed the cabin doors and started the safety announcements.

The big guy finished off his drink—a Bloody Mary, from the looks of it—and closed his tray without so much as a glance my way. The least he could have done was grab a mimosa or something for me, but nope. He'd sat his fat ass down in 2D and drank to his heart's content, waiting for the unlucky person to be seated next to him.

It was my own doing, but I was fully wedged into the outer steel armrest . . . this was my fucking luck. There was plenty of room on my oversized leather seat for my slender size 4 hips, but I was pissed and letting it show.

Perky blond number two came through and collected Biggie's empty glass without offering me anything.

"Can I get one? Or is it too late?" I pointed at the fancy airline glassware and prayed to every god I knew that she would say yes.

"After we take off."

Shit squared. The one time I desperately needed the complimentary cocktail.

Snatching my phone as we taxied to the runway, I sent my best friend, Janie, a quick text.

> Charli: *On plane, taking off, seated next to the Biggest Loser. Really. Will need a drink later.*

I powered off my phone before she could reply, twisted my hair into a messy bun, and pushed back into my seat while the captain announced we were next in line for takeoff. Closing my eyes, I squeezed them shut and giggled to myself.

Janie was probably going ballistic from my text. She could never wait patiently for the scoop. I imagined the two of us later, laughing until it hurt over cocktails, our hair blown out, stilettos on our feet, and not a worry in the world.

Then later, remorse set in. I was a grown woman, not a college coed, laughing at another human being. I shouldn't make jokes at this guy's expense, an innocent bystander I didn't even know, and I shouldn't even want to find it funny. I mentally scolded myself for acting like a spoiled Manhattan socialite until we were in the air.

That's the problem with moving too fast in life . . . you skip important stages like getting the giggles out. If I'd had a normal college career, maybe I'd be able to move forward without turning my nose up at this guy. Then again, Janie had one, and I bet she couldn't behave around this dude either.

I need a new life.

The minute we reached cruising altitude, I opened the tray, pulled out my laptop, and looked toward Ms. Perky Pants, sending her urgent mental signals for my drink.

I powered up Lucy and signed in to the back end of my work. I was an editor for *BubblePOP*, and I'd been off for a week due to my grandmother's death and funeral. Now I had a shit-ton of work to make up and my mom was going off half-cocked, trying to set me up with Garrett, my fourth cousin twice removed. He was adopted and half Asian, so it was all kosher in her mind.

"Garrett's a real catch, Char, " my mom had whispered into my ear after the funeral. "He's got a good job at some law firm, travels to all these exotic places because he's trilingual, and he's ready to settle down. Look at him. He's not bad at all, and his life is a perfect combo of wanderlust and settled. And he's going to be in New York for the next six months! You're twenty-eight . . . enough with the crazy career stuff already. Time for you to make a life with someone. It's meant to be, like Dad and me. For the right guy, I didn't mind giving up everything," she'd practically squealed in a house of mourning.

Garrett had been standing in the corner, drinking tea. When I gave him a hesitant smile, he'd practically peed himself. Bottom line, he was a dweeb loser who was smarter than most but had little to no experience with the opposite sex—except for the occasional call girl in Hong Kong, I presumed. And based on the designer Euro-trash skinny suit he was wearing, his secretary obviously dressed him.

I had zero clue as to why my mom wanted me to date him. She'd always been a free spirit and now suddenly she was all too serious. I chalked it up to my grandmother's death and shoved Garrett to the back of my mind.

"Ouch," I yelped as a sharp pain shot through my elbow and jolted me out of my daydream/nightmare.

"I'm sorry," Biggie murmured as he dragged his own laptop up to his tray after accidentally smacking me in the arm.

"It's okay," I huffed. I went back to Lucy, scrolling through recent posts in the section I oversaw.

"So, *BubblePOP*?"

My concentration was again interrupted by the large person next to me. He was leaning over the armrest and inserting himself even further into my personal space.

Actually, he smelled kind of good. Like rain and something else, maybe cinnamon. Was that his gum?

"Excuse me?" I turned my head the slightest bit so I could see him.

He had wedged one of his very large neon-green Beats noise-cancellation headphones to the side, freeing an ear, and smiled as he nodded at my screen. His smile was so honest, so endearing, I found it hard to be annoyed at his spying.

"*BubblePOP*? You know, the online megasite with Bubble in script letters and then POP in all caps? You like it? I see you're reading it." He prodded me with questions, pointing at my screen and beaming that epic smile my way the whole time.

"I do like the site. I mean, I work for them and I've been off, so I kind of have to get caught up."

Semi-reluctantly, I gave him the brush-off. We had a ninety-minute flight ahead of us and I needed to work, yet something about his confident smile made me want to chat more. But that would make me weird, right? He certainly wasn't my type, nowhere near what I'd convinced myself I needed or wanted. Or both.

"Here you go, ma'am."

The stewardess—flight attendant—handed me my drink, mocking me with a little smirk on her face. She should; I sat there with my tight smile and even more strangling attitude.

"Cheers." My seatmate good-naturedly tipped his glass toward me. He wasn't going to leave me alone.

I took a long gulp and looked back at my computer screen.

"Do you like working for them?"

I tugged at my turtleneck; it was so freaking hot all of a sudden. My nosy neighbor's face had a slight sheen to it, clearly from being hot, and now his warmth was seeping into my space.

"I do. They're a growing company and . . . I've made great strides there."

What the heck? Why was I even answering him? Because he asked, and if I was honest, it was the nicest anyone had been to me in months.

Furthermore, why did I sound like I was on an interview? Or an infomercial?

He was kind—I could tell—and his smile was gentle and calm, his eyes like warm coffee with just the right amount of cream swirling through it. I turned a little in my seat to face him and my knee brushed his thigh. I let my gaze travel his Beastie Boys T-shirt until I settled on his computer.

Playing on it was a rom-com, one I'd never seen before, but Katie What's-her-name—all stunning, shiny hair, celebrity mom, perfect life—was front and center. Her arms were full of shopping bags and she was wearing a big grin on her perfect face as she walked down a city street.

"You don't strike me as the romantic comedy type." I felt my eyebrow lift. I wasn't sure if I was teasing him or myself as the question floated from my mouth.

He laughed. It was soothing and comforting like a coffee-and-Kahlua on a cold night, and warm like the sun on the first few days of summer.

I allowed my eyes to close and imagined he looked like somebody else—not someone else totally, but just different. Fit, not slender but muscular. He still had the same gracious smile and inviting eyes, but he wasn't wearing a music T-shirt in my imagination. Maybe a Henley? And dark-wash jeans instead of the regular everyday ragged blue I'd noticed him wearing.

"It's work too," he said, interrupting my fantasy.

"Oh." I chugged the balance of my mimosa, cooling the wash of desire recently conjured up from my brain.

"Actually, I'm pretty sure *BubblePOP* will end up reviewing this one, will probably have someone at the premiere too. That's why I asked about the site. Six degrees of Kevin Bacon and all that. Our worlds are connected."

"I don't do movies. I'm the fitness editor, but if Katie What's-her-name is in it, I'm sure we'll be all over it."

He shifted his gaze over fully to me now. His eyes weren't exclusively deep brown; tiny flecks of amber circled his pupil. They were captivating in a weird way, as if they didn't belong with this guy.

I'd never met a slob who was so interesting before, yet he was definitely intriguing. And not really a slob—that was my own bias. Clearly, I was having some sort of psychotic breakdown on this airplane.

"Editor? Pretty impressive."

"Um, I'm not sure how to respond. Do I *not* look like I could be an editor?"

My claws were out. It was a bad habit of mine after years of defending my lofty goals and aptitude, a defense mechanism I should have dropped long ago. You'd think that with my lofty goals, I would be happier by now.

He ran a hand through his black hair. "I didn't mean anything by it. Just you look young enough to be a college student."

He had masculine hands, clean nails, and his hair was sort of that messy look, mussed without trying. It suited him and his whole *I don't care about my appearance* attitude. I could use a little more of that 'tude.

I shrugged. "I graduated early and took a job with another virtual rag where I did an internship. *Bubble* came for me shortly after that. I jumped at it, basically. I'd been working nonstop, round-the-clock, at the internship, and I finally felt like I was getting ahead. Now I like it; just not sure I will love it forever."

He nodded, his eyes squinting a little as he took me in, surveying not just my body—he was doing that too—but it felt more like he was trying to really see me. Get *me*. All of me.

It was an odd thing to experience after living in New York for eight years where no one truly *got* anyone. Life was spent treading on the surface—*cramps constantly making my proverbial legs ache, trying to remain afloat*—where I desperately struggled to remain at the very top, not willing to be the one to dive in. That's where the bottom-feeders were.

"So, yeah," I said. "I'm an editor."

Here I was explaining myself to a stranger, talking more about my inner self than I did to my closest friends, and I didn't even know his name. Janie would flip if she saw what I was up to, especially with this freak.

That hateful thought reminded me of my earlier text, and shame coated every cell in my body. This guy was nothing but a gentleman, and handsome if I studied him long enough. Not a freak or the Biggest Loser.

I tried to look away, busy my mind with something else, but his deep voice interrupted my thoughts. It was a tad scratchy, and I had to admit, that was sexy. I wanted to close my eyes and listen to him ask me questions.

And give him my answers, unfiltered and real—since he meant nothing to me.

"Sweet. Still, an editor. You should be proud. Wow . . . I've been doing my own gig for close to a decade. Before that I was nothing more than a glorified coffee-runner . . . that's code for intern out west. For a long time, actually, I did that. But I paid my dues and now I work for myself, doing my own thing. Know what I mean?"

"I'm sorry to say, but not really. Even with this *gig*." I used air quotes, which was not like me. I was unsettled, a bit off-kilter around this guy. "I'm still putting my time in and all that. But it's kind of cool to know there's an end of the rainbow somewhere. At least, to meet one person who's done it. I've been on the grind for so long, pushing to do everything faster and better than the next person. Was it worth it?"

I smoothed my hand over Lucy, the universal signal that I had work to do, but I didn't know if I really wanted him to leave me alone.

More emotional waves crashed around me. This guy wasn't all that bad—his voice and eyes and hands and compliments were something new to me. He was compelling me to speak the truth, to utter out loud the things that kept me awake at night. A small part of me wanted to get lost in him and whatever he was all about.

When a bout of turbulence rocked the cabin, knocking me into the dude, I was certain it was God's way of punishing me for my bitchiness.

"You okay?" He beat me to the punch before I had a chance to apologize for elbowing him in the ribs.

I nodded and took him in, surveying him longer than I should have. He wasn't so slobby. In fact, this guy looked quite organized to me. Simply put—he was overweight. Fat. Big.

And kind and endearing.

"I'm doing the music for the film. The sound track," he offered without being asked, his green headphones now completely off his ears and hanging around his neck, tinny sounds screaming from them.

I nodded again, unable to figure out why he kept talking to me. Couldn't he see how obnoxious I was? I was sure he could see through my snobbery.

"Like Jack Black in *The Holiday*," he explained. "Not just the jingles that go along with some of the scenes but all the music, song selection and sound effects, chats with music producers." He stopped short and gave me a wry grin. "I don't know why I'm talking like I'm at an interview. I do a lot, and I love what I do. It's kind of my dream."

"Nice," I finally answered. He wasn't goofy-looking like Jack. Actually, his face was a bit more defined and handsome, and his eyes were the kindest I'd ever seen. I could get lost inside them for a lifetime . . . Well, if the rest of the whole package was right for me.

"So, you're going home? New York?" he asked, peppering me with questions once again. We'd been chatting so long, my laptop winked out, going to sleep.

"Home for me. Now, anyway. Originally, I'm from here . . . or Chicago where we took off from."

"Got it. Family stuff?"

"Funeral. My grandmother." *Why am I even answering this dude?*

"Sorry to hear. I actually live in LA, but I couldn't get a direct flight to New York."

I was tempted to say, "I didn't ask," like I normally would to cut someone off. But for some reason, this guy was winning me over.

"It's spring break. I had a hard time getting a decent flight too," I said instead.

"I'm Layton, by the way."

Layton? Was this guy for real? Was he a soap opera star who got cut and ended up nearly eating himself to death?

There I went again with the bitchiness.

I looked up at his eyes and all my mean thoughts slipped away. I wanted to be rude, but there was something about this guy.

"Charli," I said. "It's Charleston, really, but who names their daughter after a city in South Carolina?"

Layton continued to focus his award-winning smile on me, the corners of his eyes crinkling with contained laughter. "Really?"

I nodded and ran my hand over the top of my laptop, finally closing the screen. It was clear I wasn't going to get any work done on the flight.

"Yep. My dad was in a band and their last gig was in Charleston, where he met my mom. She was there for some spring break thing with her roommate—they were professional groupies, made a life out of traveling and spring breaking, chasing down indie bands. They'd gone to some bar and the rest is history. It was a last hurrah for my dad, anyway. He was heading out to Chicago to shackle himself to a job in the hospitality industry."

"Wow." Layton turned a bit more in his seat, as much as his width would allow him to do. "Did he ever play music again?" He tilted his head and put all his focus on me.

"He used to tinker around with it when I was little, but not really play-play after that night. He'd gone to Cornell Hotel School . . . it's a pretty big deal. *He* was a pretty big deal, I guess. Dad was a force of his own, and he was determined to skip working in the boonies at some motel. He went straight to the five-star places, the four-diamond establishments, and landed a job. I guess he straddled me with his need to be the best, and then he died. My mom stayed the course after he was gone, pushing me to do what he would have wanted."

Here I was again, spilling everything to the guy seated next to me on an airplane. A man named Layton who looked nothing like the alpha suits I met in the city, but was growing on me.

"Want another?" Layton pointed at the empty champagne flute in my hand, the one I hadn't noticed I was still holding.

"Sure."

He pressed the button for Ms. Perky, and she appeared with a notepad in hand.

"Two more." Layton pointed at my barren glass and added, "Whatever she was having and a merrrry . . . me—" A sudden jolt shook us in our seats, and then he finished, "Mary for me, of course."

The turbulence jolted me back to reality, or maybe it was the last part of what he said. I wasn't sure I'd heard him correctly, but it was a dose of reality either way.

"Merry me?" Confused, I repeated what I'd heard, emphasizing the rolling *r*'s.

"Mary, as in Bloody Mary," he said, correcting me.

"Oh, ugh. I'm so tired. I heard *merry me* and I thought you meant . . . I don't know . . . me or something. Never mind." I let out a nervous giggle.

What was happening to me? It was as if cheerleaders had taken over my mind and body like the aliens did in that one movie.

"Merry as in this is the best plane ride I've had in a long time? Absolutely, it is. And I may have been insinuating my being very lucky to have a cocktail with you, but no marriage necessary."

He set his hand lightly on my arm, capturing my attention and sending spirals of friction through my sleeve, and my eyes widened.

"Oh," he said quickly. "This was a merry moment until a second ago. I'm sorry if I offended you."

A blush swept up my neck, thankfully hidden by my turtleneck. This all getting to be too much . . . the want, need, and disgust all rolled up in one big wad of *no thank you*. I didn't do emotions like this. I was practical, matter-of-fact, lived my life in absolutes. Black and white was always more comfortable for me.

At the end of the day, that was why I was an editor. I lived by the rules—in life, work, friendships, and relationships. There were certain dictates to live by and I followed them. Never mind that I didn't know who the hell came up with those rules; I still followed them like they were a doctrine.

"Don't answer," he said kindly, letting me off the hook. "I am lucky. Anybody would be lucky sitting next to you. So what if we're stuck sitting next to each other on a plane? I'm still lucky."

My cheeks burned. "I didn't mean it like that."

"It's cool, Charli, New York's a big place. When we get off this flying piece of metal, you never have to see me again."

I didn't respond. The words got all tangled up in my vocal cords, and shame covered me like snow falling on the skating rink at Rockefeller Center.

"Here you go." The attendant set our drinks down in front of us.

Not knowing what else to say, I went back to Lucy, and Layton returned his gaze to Katie What's-her-name and her big happy-go-lucky smile.

Two

Layton

Two Days Later

I handed the woman at the gate my ticket and headed down the Jetway to the airplane that would take me back to LA. Seven o'clock in the morning felt like the middle of the night to me since I hadn't adjusted to East Coast time. I cursed myself for not grabbing a decent cup of coffee and for not waiting to take a later flight. Maybe I would have been able to get a first-class seat on it.

Finally, I stepped onto the plane and shuffled to my row. To make matters worse, I was in a middle seat. Locating 14B, I shoved my bag in the overhead bin and said, "Excuse me," to the slim grandmotherly woman already seated in the aisle seat.

"Of course," she said, and smiled as she stood to let me through.

Unfortunately, the dude in 14A didn't look as nice or as happy.

I couldn't help but think of Charli and her initial reaction to sitting next to me. Quickly shoving thoughts of the mysterious attractive woman to the back of my mind, I wedged myself into the middle seat.

Of course, the fucking cowhand in the window seat piped up, wearing a smug look along with his tight jeans, flannel shirt, cowboy hat, and boots.

"We thought we were gonna get some skinny New Yorker here," he drawled. "No such luck."

I refused to hang my head in shame. I was a good person, as good as anyone. I'd always been stocky, and my mom's cooking didn't help. At that thought, I made a mental note to visit my parents in the nursing home.

Their being older than my friends' parents didn't help either. Mom and Dad didn't do all the active stuff other parents did with their kids. Instead, we enjoyed family movie night with popcorn and candy. It's probably why I went into the movie business like I did.

"You got it, my man. No such luck," I said to the cowboy, keeping my tone light.

I was used to pricks like him. Been dealing with them since puberty, when some kids lost their baby fat and others didn't. I did have a few years in college where I'd slimmed down due to playing a lot of ultimate Frisbee on the lawn with my roommates and hitting the weight room. But after graduation I moved out on my own, and frankly, I ate when I was bored or lonely.

And even when I wasn't. The fact was, I enjoyed food. It reminded me of home.

I buckled up and pulled out my phone to check my messages. *Look at that . . . I don't even need the seat-belt expander. So take that, asshole.*

"What'd you do? Eat the island of Manhattan?" my seatmate said with a mean-spirited chuckle.

This asshole wasn't going to let it go.

Neither was I.

"Excuse me, I have to grab something from my bag," I said to the grandmother next to me, who unbuckled her seat belt and stood in the aisle with an embarrassed smile on her face as I grabbed my headphones and laptop.

What with the close quarters, I hadn't planned on working, but this guy warranted my headphones. I squeezed back in my seat, Grandma sat back down, and Cowboy muttered another grumble. I opened my laptop on my lap, plugged in, and set about ignoring my flying partner.

For a second, I thought about making some changes to myself. I could go to Weight Watchers or some shit, but why? At home I had friends, women, and coworkers who didn't dismiss me.

Only two people had done that recently. The second one, I couldn't give two shits about. But the first one mattered. I'd gone and hurt her, although unintentionally, so maybe I deserved the tiny bit of shame Charli had made me feel when she first stepped on the plane.

It was exhilarating to watch her come alive in front of me, let go of her preconceived notions for a moment and talk to me like a real person, even sharing her inner thoughts with me. I'd wanted to reach out and brush back the small wisps of hair that had worked their way free from her bun and tell her to follow her dreams.

But I didn't. Instead I'd gone and made a mess of it.

I felt a jab in my shoulder and looked toward the culprit, reluctantly pushing back one of my earphones so I could hear his nonsense.

"If you're gonna sit there and watch that gay-love shit," he growled out, "I'm getting off the plane."

Confused for a second, I looked back to my screen. On it was a scene from an old movie I'd worked on . . . two men having a tense romantic stare-down in a club. Mushroom jazz blared in the background as their eyes warred with each other. It had recently been nominated for an MTV award, so I was re-watching it.

"Shut the fuck up, dude," was all I responded and went back to the screen.

I'd had enough of him.

Sadly, I didn't get enough of Charli.

Three

Charli

One Week Later

I pushed through the revolving door, rain dripping off my jacket as I made my way into the Royal Hotel. Shaking my hair out, I took in the obnoxious grand lobby, all marble and brass, but this was where Janie worked. Despite its staid atmosphere, the Royal seemed to be the place to meet people lately, although I never met anyone worth meeting.

"Hey there, Char." Craig the bartender greeted me as I grabbed a stool at the bar. "The usual?"

"Hey there, and yes, please."

He poured a generous amount of red wine and set the glass in front of me. I heard Janie before I saw her—her loud heels clicking the floor.

"Hiya, girl!" Janie bent down from her gargantuan five-foot-eleven frame, her jet-black hair cascading over her shoulder, and kissed my cheek.

"Hey, J-babe." I pinched her cheek and she swatted my hand away.

"Don't touch! My makeup is perfect; had it done today in the gift shop."

"It does look good, love the eyeliner. Is it glittery?"

"You know it!" Janie batted her long eyelashes at me, her glossy red lips forming a perfect smile.

Craig set a vodka gimlet in front of Janie, and she tossed him an air kiss and an exaggerated wink.

That was Janie, all kisses and hugs and PDA, no matter who it was. Her last boyfriend couldn't deal with all the attention bestowed upon him, let alone everyone else she knew. Now she was single and doing a bang-up job of feeling up every man she met . . . *up and down.* I was surprised she didn't hurl her Bond-girl body over the bar and into Craig's arms.

"Fab haircut, Charleston."

I rolled my eyes at the mention of my formal name.

"Love it. It's so chic and in, whatever." She ran her fingers through the ends of my dark blond hair.

"It's just a few long layers, but yeah, it does feel better. Lighter. Who knows if I'll be able to style it by myself." I took a sip of my wine, the burgundy liquid warming my belly. "And I got stuck in the rain, trying to get a cab, so it probably resembles a rat right now."

"It's got this whole ratty-yet-seductive Selena Gomez thing going on," Janie said. "But not dark, of course. It's good. The color is perfect, blond honey and chestnut. Blech, I hate that it's natural, you bitch." She whispered the last part, still twisting her fingers in my hair. "You know what? You should hook up tonight!"

Unfortunately, that part she didn't whisper. She always went straight to the hook-up thing.

Always.

But it had to be hooking up with the *right guy.* The Wall Street one or the surgeon from the Upper East Side or the guy we knew in college who invented a million widgets. I didn't know who or what the hell I wanted, yet I continued to buy into Janie's mindset.

Did I even deserve anyone like that? How could I be worthy of someone?

Would someone feel worthy of supporting me in what I really wanted to do?

And what the heck *did* I want to do? I didn't have a clue.

I took a long sip of my wine, needing to soothe the ache in my belly.

Watching my mom flit through life after my dad passed, unable to move on while only obsessing more over me, that was no life. Hearing her talk about life before my dad—the bands, the excitement, and her fellow groupies—that was her passion, her mission, a manifesto of sorts that she abandoned when she fell for my dad. To me, that life seemed so strange, to flit and float around after musicians, but it was still her life.

Then I found myself in a front-row seat, watching her after my dad passed. Her life before, during, and after him was like scattered pieces from random puzzles, none of them fitting with one another.

But me, I wanted something different. Not her before or after or anything like her life as I ever knew it.

"Please. I haven't hooked up since months ago, and that guy wanted to use a butt plug on the first date. No, thank you."

Janie took a seductive sip of her drink through the stirrer straw and waggled her eyebrows. "Seriously, Char, you may like a butt plug. With the perfect guy."

"Maybe . . . after I know a man for more than a dinner."

"Eh, knowing a guy is overrated."

"So, what's going on with you?" I quickly changed the subject, steering it far away from butt plugs.

"Well, my boss is a dick but this job pays well, so fuck it. He's got me running all over town for some traveling-dinner thing he wants to sponsor as part of New York Restaurant Week. He's practically salivating to be the sponsor hotel. I'm going to blow up like the Goodyear blimp with all the places he has me eating."

"Aw, poor baby. Did you have to shove down brunch at Balthazar and burgers at Minetta?"

"As a matter of fact, I did. And I haven't gotten laid in weeks. Must be all the extra pounds."

"La-la-la, I'm not listening. You're a beanpole, and I have to work the spinner bike like it's a stripper pole. Although I lost some weight last week when I was home."

Janie brought her thumb to my cheek and caressed my skin, her demeanor immediately changing. That was the thing about her—she was bitchy and bossy and self-centered, and dramatic. Maybe some would say narcissistic, but she was good to the core.

"How are you with all of that? I should be checking in more, but last week when you first got home, you seemed cool. Should I be bringing soup or whatever? Matzah ball? Mishmash? I'll call my *bubbe* and ask where to get the best."

Her soft, shiny, poker-straight black hair (thanks to the salon and those foul-smelling chemicals) whisked around my face as she came in to hug me tight, squeezing the ever-loving life out of me. I shoved her off after allowing her to hold on to me for an extra second.

"Gram was ninety-two," I said, "and I'm fine. She lived a big, long, full life. And no, don't bother your *bubbe*. She's probably involved in a week-long Mahj tournament, and doesn't need to worry about soup."

"By the way, if I start to play Mah-jongg, call the loony bin." Janie constantly worried she would turn into the stereotypical Upper-East New Yorker like her mom.

"Of course. But seriously, last week it was my mom making me nuts, and she's still at it. Can you believe she's still trying to fix me up with Garrett, my half-Asian distant cousin? She's so obsessed with me making a life, settling down. I think she forgets what it was like when she did it. She's like a heat-seeking missile when it comes to marrying me off. Sometimes I'm afraid to go home for fear he's hanging around on my stoop, waiting for me."

Janie lifted an eyebrow. "Maybe you should move?"

I burst out laughing. Hiccups ensued and happy tears rolled from my eyes.

"Move? No way! I would never leave my rent-controlled place. Ever. But this is just so strange with my mom. She lived a nomad's life before my dad, and now she's so determined to see me settled . . . with your type of guy. Are you two talking? Working together?"

The thought of moving was laughable enough, let alone doing it for a guy like Garrett, and Janie knew it. I'd fought like a bride in Filene's Basement to get that condo. I would die there.

Alone—probably.

And that was pretty much how the rest of the evening went. Laughs, Janie rubbing up against multiple men, and more laughs.

Later, I crawled into bed, fluffed my pillows, and turned on Lucy.

I scanned my in-box for work stuff. Warm weather was quickly approaching, so the next few months would be a flurry of articles and features on flat stomachs, staying hydrated during outdoor summer exercise routines, and staying bikini-ready.

My team was champing at the bit to get a feature story. Poor Maggie, my newest intern, had sent me twelve pitches, not one of them original. The subject lines ranged from *Legs and Lunges in Central Park* to *Staying Swimsuit Fab on the High Line.* We'd done those articles every summer. They were filler, stuffed onto the pages of *BubblePOP* when we didn't have anything better—which was less and less often with me. I was upping my game.

I wrote back to Maggie, encouraging her to think outside the box, check out new trends, and come up with something fresher, hinting at a few untapped topics. Something that would get eyeballs on our site, lots of them.

I ignored the e-mail from my mom with nothing in the subject line. I knew it was a Garrett-fueled message.

The next e-mail was from my boss, Larissa. There was a staff meeting later this week, and I was expected to have a full report.

I clicked into my spam folder; I checked it once a day. I'd learned my lesson the hard way when Brooke Burke was trying to get a hold of me and her message went to spam. For some unknown reason, I decided to check the folder and there it was, luckily only a day after she sent it. That feature went wild; every woman over thirty who wanted to look like Burke clicked on it.

Of course, there wasn't much tonight. I tossed a bunch of sale e-mails from J. Crew, Athleta, and Amazon into the trash folder until only one was left.

FROM: LaytonG@darksidemusictracks.com
TO: Charleston_Richards@BubblePOP.com
SUBJECT: Apology

Dear Charleston –

Before you wonder, yes, I stalked you and found you, but only to say I'm sorry. I swear! Although there aren't too many fitness editors named Charleston around, so you're a pretty easy target.

Peggy over at *BubblePOP* was kind enough to give me your e-mail (I sort of lied and said I had a big Hollywood pitch and then offered movie passes to Katie's film).

Well, I'm rambling like I did on the plane, and I by no means meant to offend you when I said "Merry Mary" or admitted to being lucky. I also would have much rather spent the flight chatting with you than looking at Katie.

I guess it was for the best because you had a lot to catch up on. Again, I'm sorry about your grandma. And my actions.

I had a good time in New York, but I kept thinking it would have been better if you were able to connect for a drink. I held back in writing until I left.

Look me up if you ever get to LA.

Good luck in all you do—

Wow, an editor. You should be proud, but don't sacrifice what you really want.

—Lay(ton) Griffin

Holy shit! What the heck is this?

I slapped Lucy closed and turned out my light, curled under my down comforter (perfectly purple, more lavender actually), and closed my eyes.

"Lay" had written to me after I'd been such a bitch, and I'd slammed my laptop closed without so much as a reply. What was with him? We sat next to each other on a plane, his forehead shiny and his thigh touching mine, and not in a sexual way.

Fuckity-fuck. Why did I have to go and give him my name? Now he's freaking finding me and acting all nice when I don't deserve it.

I sat up, clicked the light back on, and grabbed my remote. No way was I going to sleep now. I turned on my TV that sits on top of my antique white chiffonier and scrolled through the movies. *How to Win a Guy in a Month* came on the screen.

Double what the fuck? Katie was everywhere I turned.

Of course, I fluffed my lilac pillows and settled in to watch. After all, this was my specialty . . . losing a guy. If I could even get a guy, other than Layton, clearly a big Star Wars fan . . .

Dark Side Music? Ha. Please.

I'm a twenty-eight-year-old editor in the Big Apple with everything going for me. I'm a catch, right?

Then why did this stranger make my spine tingle and my heart warm?

I didn't know him from the next guy, and he wasn't close to my type. Yet his eyes made me want to ditch my stilettos and jump in, feet first.

Four

Charli

When my alarm went off, I rolled out of bed and checked my phone for the temperature outside. After pulling on my favorite burgundy lululemon leggings and a Nike fleece jersey, I quickly put on socks and shoes, grabbed my headphones, and ran out the door. On the elevator to the lobby, I hit the button for my grunge playlist and secured my phone in my armband. As soon as the doors opened, I jogged to the front door and out into the chilly early spring weather.

I lived in an old warehouse in the Meatpacking District that had been converted into condos, and I'd been there since the revitalization started. It wasn't the Village but it was loud and vibrant, the place to live if you were young and on the up-and-up. I loved it. My condo was close to the High Line, and all mine. My first place was nothing more than a glorified closet with a bathroom, but now I had a one-bedroom with high factory ceilings and exposed brick-and-metal walls in the middle of the coolest neighborhood in New York.

I picked up speed as my feet struck the pavement, making my way to the Line without even having to think about it. I did this four or five days a week, usually Monday through Wednesday, Friday and Sunday, with yoga on Thursday and Saturday. If I wasn't running, I went spinning.

Hey, I was a fitness editor. Practice what you preach and all that. Plus, my sanity depended on it. It was the only way to mentally run away from the demons that haunted me. My fitness schedule was like a salve for my broken soul.

This morning I tried to stay focused on my music, but my mind kept wandering to a pair of rich brown eyes, compassionate and considerate. I wondered where he was from. Not New York or LA for sure, not with his kind manner.

Layton.

All night I'd felt compelled to answer his message, but had resisted the urge. Why should I? I was never going to see him again.

At the end of the day, I slumped at my desk, staring at my steaming large coffee from Dean and DeLuca and the half-eaten bran muffin discarded next to it. My body spent, I was desperate to go home and slip into lounge pants.

Except I still had one more unpleasant task to handle, a part of my job I didn't necessarily like and often felt I was too young to do, but that was just an excuse. Sadly, it came with the territory, so I pulled on my big-girl undies and picked up the phone.

"Maggie, can you come here?"

My intern flitted in like she was the boss, confident her ideas were the best I'd ever heard.

"Sit down, Maggie."

She plopped down in the chair across from my desk like we were colleagues, flipping her bright red shawl of hair over her shoulder as she said, "What's up?"

She really said it just like that. Seriously. Like we were happy-hour buddies.

"Maggie, it's come to my attention you've been pitching ideas to our main competitor as well as a bunch of other Internet outlets while interning here." When she opened her mouth to protest, I held up a hand to shush her. "Yes, if you were freelance, that would be okay. But you have a non-compete during the term of your internship."

It was a mouthful made in corporate speak, another part of the job I despised. The lingo sucked every last creative cell from my body.

"I wasn't trading secrets or anything, just trying to get an article, Charl-eee." She sounded like my mom did lately, whiny and malcontent.

I didn't mind being on a first-name basis with my intern, but the way my name rolled off her tongue like we were BFFs irked me. I mentally chastised myself for only being twenty-eight and not worthy of respect, as if it were my fault.

In a surprising and unwanted train of thought, my mind drifted to Layton and his reaction to my position as an editor. He'd practically laughed when I said I was an editor. *Or did he?*

"Maggie, listen, I don't make the policies, and I know you desperately want to get your name out there, but this isn't how to do it. You're bright, but I think you're trying too hard. I'm not entirely certain you're not pitching the entire island of Manhattan. Maybe spreading yourself too thin?"

"Char, seriously, I'm cool. I'll stop." Maggie's blue eyes were wide and innocent, sparkling even, not concerned and contrite like they should have been for a lowly intern being chastised as she was.

Time to put the hammer down.

"I have to let you go, Maggie. I'm sorry. It's been a pleasure mentoring you while you were here, but now it's time for you to go. I wish it were different, but you violated our agreement and the lawyers upstairs have a zero-tolerance policy."

More corporate babble from me, and yet not a shred of humility on her part.

"That's bull—" she spat out, then cooled her jets a little. "I'm a damn good intern, Charli." Refusing to stand, she braced her hands on the armrest as she argued with me.

"It is what it is, Maggie. Stay in touch."

I turned my attention to Lucy, making out like I had a million other tasks to do, but I was done. I was exhausted and my ego was bruised. Even Maggie didn't take me seriously; she could see right through my facade. My outer shell might be New York chic, all stilettos and toughness, but inside I was trembling.

As Maggie stood in a huff and stomped out of my office, I leaned back in my chair and took a long slug of my coffee. The hot liquid made creamy with two-percent milk warmed my stomach and eased the headache that was building behind my eyes.

I was supposed to meet up with Janie again after work, but that wasn't going to happen. I still had two stories to approve and it was late; the windows had already grown dark. Sighing, I closed out the windows on my screen, resigned to dragging Lucy home with me yet again.

Was this what I wanted? I wasn't even writing anymore, just slashing my virtual red pen across the writing of others. My current reality seemed like a pale comparison to my old dreams.

Shoving my dissatisfaction to the back of my mind, I forged ahead with my routine. It was definitely a hail-a-cab kind of evening, and the salad bar around the corner was calling to me. They had the best tuna salad in New York.

But my hands had a mind of their own and didn't power Lucy down. Instead, I pulled up my spam folder.

Needing to busy my hands while it loaded, I twisted my hair as best I could. It was half ponytail, half messy bun, and mostly falling out of the elastic band since my hair was shorter now.

My fingers worked over my mouse, hurriedly deleting all the sales pitches and requests for money to be sent to foreign lands, and then they began typing.

FROM: Charleston_Richards@BubblePOP.com
TO: LaytonG@darksidemusictracks.com
SUBJECT: Re: Apology

Layton –

Thank you so much for your kind words. But seriously, there was no need. ~~We were just neighbors on a flight, and you don't owe me anything.~~

Oh God. I'm hitting backspace more than actually writing.

We were airline companions, both under deadlines. I enjoyed your company while we chatted, ~~and I wish you luck in your endeavors.~~

I hope the movie does awesome! Of course, ~~I am going to try to snag a ticket to the premiere now that I met you~~ I am going to definitely see it when it comes out and will look for your name in the credits.

Be well, and one of these days, I hope to visit LA. ~~and will e-mail you.~~

Thanks again for your condolences.

Best wishes,

Charli

I hit SEND before I second-guessed what I was doing, smacked Lucy closed with gusto, and decided to order Chinese.

I was no longer in the mood to be good and eat a salad. Instead I was disgusted with myself for chasing after someone, for making a fool of myself with a man who shouldn't matter, and I wanted to sulk in pan-fried noodles.

As I made my way out of my office, my stiletto boots beating quietly on the carpet, I saw a note taped on my assistant's desk.

Charli –

I knew you were busy with Maggie and I didn't want to interrupt, but this arrived for you at the end of the day.
—Cecilia

Next to the handwritten Post-it note was an enormous bouquet of flowers arranged in an oversized champagne flute.

A second handwritten note was stuck inside the pink-and-purple potpourri of wildflowers. Not trite roses or friendly carnations, something way better and unique. In the wild, they'd be considered weeds, but here in this elegant arrangement, they were groomed and gorgeous.

Charli-

Making sure you got my e-mail.

Apologies again.

Hope you're popping bubbles . . . or whatever it is you do at work. Dotting i's and crossing t's, I guess.

—Layton

Like the flowers, I'd first dismissed their sender as a weed in the wild, but once I'd cut through the rough . . .

Ugh.

This wasn't the time to get poetic. Or to mix metaphors.

I would have to add an ice cream on the street (*maybe eat it first?*) to my Chinese splurge.

Flowers? For me? I was the one who should be apologizing, not him.

And the champagne glass? He really seemed to know the way to my heart.

Not to mention his voice, which rang in my ear all the way home. I took the subway in an effort to drown out my imagining his sandpapery voice reading his note aloud. I stood there, clutching my floral arrangement over my bag across my chest, thinking a cab would have been better but I needed the distraction.

It didn't work, though. In my mind, Layton's eyes were fixed on me and really seeing me, checking my reaction. His inspection of me felt real, sending tingles over my skin and need clawing down my spine. I itched to see Layton in real life and not only in my mind, which was so strange considering I'd only met him once.

Finally, we arrived at my stop. I sent up a silent prayer of thanks as the bustle of exiting the subway station and holding on to my present was enough to put an end to my overactive imagination.

Five

Layton

I sat on my patio, my feet up on the table and a beer in my hand, the night quiet except for Harriette's rustling around in the yard. I shut my eyes and breathed in the salty air.

Why did I have to go and send flowers? And I don't mean calling up 1-800-Flowers like some dumb bachelor. No, I'd googled for the most highly recommended boutique florist in New York City and called them up myself.

"I need something special for someone . . . unique," I'd said over the phone. "A one-off, rich in colors and, hmmm, let me think. In a champagne glass?"

The guy with an accent told me he could work with that, and set about e-mailing me a picture of an oversized champagne glass and a quote. I'd responded right away with an affirmative.

Okay, before you start handing out awards for "Dude of the Year," I must admit, I'd seen this move in a movie. It was a romantic dramedy where the guy never seemed to get the girl he wanted until . . . he really tried.

Story of my life, really.

I'd had a ton of women. Gingers, brunettes, and even a few Asians. I liked them all. They liked me too. I was funny and I set them at ease. They weren't perfect. Too skinny, heads covered with overly curly hair, they loved the Jedi Force or enjoyed graphic novels—those were my kind of girl. Around me, they felt good about themselves, at ease and confident. They complimented me and meant it.

I was self-made, successful, and a bit of a romantic. All those characteristics were in my favor. And my personality wasn't so bad, I'd been told. I listened to people, really listened, and I was generous. In and out of bed.

Although I'd been told this, I'd never gotten *the girl*, the one everyone else wanted. And the minute I saw Charli walk onto the plane, I knew she was *that* kind of girl. The one everyone wanted.

Yeah, she tried to hide behind the bitchy attitude, the New York snobbery, but for a minute or five, I broke her down. I saw behind her prissy shell and couture armor, and I wanted that. All of that.

"I did, my pretty lady," I said to my only true girl. "I saw it and broke her down."

Actually, my one-and-only sat at my side, panting from chasing after her ball and dripping drool onto my knee. I shifted in my seat, wincing when my cargo shorts bit into my ass, and sighed at the sight of my T-shirt clinging to my stomach—a reminder of why my dog was my only girl.

On a long exhale, I told myself I should settle for one of the women who found me appealing, inside and out, rather than chase the unattainable. But I couldn't stop my mind from conjuring up images of Charli, or running away with the idea of seeing her again.

I had a plan.

If she'd only e-mail me back.

Harriette looked at me like *What the fuck?* Her soft doggie eyes were so droopy and inviting, and even though she adored me, even she didn't believe I had a chance.

"Here's to hoping the flowers help. Come on, girl." I stood, patted Harriette on the head, and went back inside the house.

Six

Charli

"Charli! Over here. Charli!"

Janie waved at me from a far corner of the crowded bar at Chowww. It was her birthday, and she insisted we celebrate here. The place was loud, trendy, and expensive, so it was no surprise.

"Hey, girl, happy birthday!" I squeezed her tight and kissed her cheek, wedging myself into the small space next to her and the bar.

She leaned close, raising her voice so I could hear. "Craig is going to stop by, and Haley, Shani, and Bianca are all coming."

"Well, I get to buy you your first drink. What are you going to have?"

I motioned for the bartender, a sexy brunette with her hair slicked back in a long ponytail and thick eyeliner accentuating her eyes.

"Cucumber martini," Janie yelled over the black lacquer bar, and I chimed in, "Prosecco."

When we had our drinks, I clinked the rim of mine to hers. "Cheers."

Once we'd each had a sip, I yelled over the music, "So, you ready for a great year? Last year in your twenties."

"You know it." She twirled around in her tight spot, her eyes taking in everything around her, but I knew what she was doing.

"Stop," I said.

"Oh, come on. I'm just looking for a few prospects."

"Do not include me in your list of available women."

"Why not? You look smoking. Plus, it's my birthday and I'll do what I want." To make her point, she gestured at my black blouse and skinny jeans. "I mean, really, Char. No one wears a tight blouse like that and painted-on dark jeans with stiletto ankle boots if they're not on the prowl."

Deflecting, I said, "Speaking of which, you look hot. Love those leather pants." Janie was in skintight red leather pants and a white frilly blouse. "And look at those shoes!" Preening, she lifted a foot in the air and twisted her ankle from side to side, and I grinned. "They're definitely perfectly cheetah."

"What am I going to do with you, girl?" She pinched my cheek and winked. "Perfectly cheetah . . . ha! You've talked that way since I've known you. Probably since birth."

We sipped at our drinks for a moment while some Euro-synthesized rap-style music blared in the background, the bass vibrating all the way through me.

"Oh, there's Bianca," she said. "Don't tell her we're going spinning on Sunday. She'll want to go and then beg to go to a later class, and we'll never make brunch or see *him*."

"Janie, my love, I don't think we have to intentionally leave her out. Not to mention, no one wants to go to spinning class before the sun is up on a Sunday."

Proud of myself, I tried inserting a small life lesson there. Janie was my closest friend, after all, and that was like a marriage. You accepted a person in sickness and health and everything in between—bitchiness included. And she was technically older in years, which I equated with experience.

Janie was an early-to-rise freak—like five o'clock every damn morning. She did more before seven than most people did all day. I'd agreed to go to a spinning class with her on Sunday at six. Apparently the teacher was a god and she had a thing for him.

"Hey there, ladies," Bianca crooned over the music, air kissing both of us and waving her bracelet-clad arm in the air. Her blond hair was sleek and straight, her makeup pristine complete with red lips, and she wore a wrap dress on her size 2 body.

Suddenly a herd of men surrounded us, offering to buy her a cocktail. She zeroed in on one rich-looking Wall Street type and said, "Sure, a lemon drop," batting her fake eyelashes the whole time.

Bianca wasn't my favorite but she was another friend of Janie's from high school, and I didn't see her much. She worked for her parents' jewelry business and sold couples expensive jewels crafted from the rainbow of happiness. The one that follows getting engaged.

Janie and I met in college in upstate New York. I was a junior credits-wise but a freshman age-wise. I couldn't go to bars or anything, so I'd been sitting in some coffee shop listening to indie rock one evening and Janie had strolled in with her posse, giggling and carefree. She gravitated toward me, probably wanting to fix me and make me happy. That's Janie. She loves a good fixer-upper project.

We'd been friends ever since, even after I graduated and moved to Manhattan. I was so happy when she moved back after graduating. Now I was a regular fixture in her social life; pretending to love it had become my specialty.

The rest of the night passed in a blur of cocktails, sushi, birthday cake, and dancing. Bianca left with the rich dude, Janie found herself a lawyer—Jewish to boot—and I shared a cab with Shani and Haley back to the Meatpacking District.

Once again, I found myself snuggled up in bed with Lucy on my lap, the heat from her fan the only thing warming my legs.

It had been a week since I'd fired Maggie, but I had my daily e-mail from her begging for her position back. There was an e-mail from one of our junior writers with a fairly interesting pitch on juicing and dating, and how the two mix or don't. And one more message, which no longer filtered into my spam folder.

FROM: LaytonG@darksidemusictracks.com
TO: Charleston_Richards@BubblePOP.com

Hi, Charli –

Thanks for getting back to me. Sorry it took me so long to reply, but we went into the last week of production on *Seven Sins of Serial Dating*, and I barely came up for air. It's a pretty decent movie for a chick flick and all that fun stuff.

There's no way to say this without it being weird, so I'm just going to ask.

I was wondering if you wanted to go to the premiere? It may be presumptuous to ask, but I could leave some tickets for you. You may even think I'm nuts for asking.

Seriously, it's funny, all good laughs, and I thought it would be great for you to get away to see it.

Let me know.

No obligation.

—Lay

What the hell was that? Come to the premiere? Did he mean with him? By myself?

And what was with the "Lay?"

Seven

Two Weeks Later

"Go to Drybar, get your hair done, and make sure you throw a pair of clean panties in your purse," Janie said over the phone.

"I'm not going to sleep with him. I don't even know if I'll see him or talk to him. Plus—"

"I didn't mean him. Who knows who you'll meet at this thing, Char? O.M.G." She spelled out the letters . . . for real. "You may see Ryan Reynolds. Make sure your bra and panties match."

I rolled my eyes and shifted my feet, avoiding a ticklish spot.

"You pick color yet?" the nail tech asked, interrupting my conversation.

"J—what should I wear? The red dress by Chanel or the black Givenchy? I think the black is safe."

"The red, definitely."

"Hold on," I said into the phone and directed my next words to the nail tech sitting at my feet. "Let's just do a French on my toes."

"Don't do a French," Janie yelled in my ear. "It looks like fingers on your feet. And you don't want that if you end up in bed with some guy."

"Janie, may I remind you I'm going for work? If Sherri hadn't come down with the stomach flu, I wouldn't be going at all."

"Not true. Your pen pal invited you."

I'd made the mistake of coming clean to Janie at brunch on Sunday after spinning . . . I must have been dehydrated or something. I told her all about my plane ride home, about Layton, and about how we occasionally corresponded over e-mail.

Our virtual chats had only become a regular thing over the last two weeks when he started working on a new project. He began sending me little clips and jokes under the guise of wanting to make me laugh after hurting my feelings. I had declined his offer to attend the premiere, saying deadlines were keeping me grounded in New York, but then Sherri got sick.

An interoffice plea for one of us to drop everything and fly to Los Angeles to cover the premiere made its way through the office, and in a weak moment, I'd agreed to go. Of course, my boss let me raid the fashion closet, including allowing me to keep the Blahniks I picked out, and off I went to California.

"Hello? Are you there, Char?"

"Yeah, I got distracted with the colors. I wasn't going to go when *Layton* invited me."

"You're there now, so time to party, babe. I want to hear every detail, and don't do the French—"

"Okay, okay."

"And don't forget the underwear in your purse."

"Good-bye, Janie."

Once I ended the call, I told the nail tech, "You know what? Let's go with that dark gray shimmery color," and leaned back into the vibrating chair.

I spent ten minutes trying to clear my head to no avail when my phone pinged with an e-mail alert. Unable to ignore the ding, I pressed the mail icon and wished I hadn't.

The first message glaring at me was from my mom, and I silently wished it had gone to spam.

Of course, she still had an AOL account. Who the heck still used America Online? My mom. Her e-mail address was ancient, a relic from her groupie days. She had no reason to part with it since she didn't really use it much. Except to bug me. I tended not to argue with her on these matters, but I was starting to think it was time we had a conversation.

I had always felt some strange sense of guilt when it came to my mom. First, she'd given up her groupie lifestyle to be with my dad. I didn't quite get her earlier choices because they seemed so opposed to how she tried to be now, but she was my mom and had sacrificed a big chunk of who she was for the privilege.

We weren't supposed to get everything our moms did, which was fine because I truly didn't. Believe me, understanding her wasn't easy. I was the resident nerd, the smart girl who was pushed ahead because my teachers couldn't teach me alongside the *regular* kids my age.

Sighing, I clicked on the message to see what she had to say.

FROM: CoolRoadie@aol.com
TO: Charleston_Richards@BubblePOP.com

Charli, darling, I understand you're in California. I called your office and learned you're not there. Obviously, I wish you would've told me. I'm not going to call you because of the time change, and because you might be working. We all know you're set on being some major career woman, and don't you forget it either!

I loved your dad, and you're just like him. He'd be so proud, which is why I hope you meet up with Garrett in NYC. He would have liked that too. Dad, I mean.

Please don't be rude.

Love you,

Mom

P.S. Call me!!

I'd call her later. Much later. Like when I got back to New York and was too swamped to meet Garrett. I dashed off a quick e-mail in response, saying I loved her back and yes, my job was extremely important to me.

Is it?

Then I scrolled down through the rest of my e-mails.

Work, big sale at Bloomies, schedule change at the spin studio, and . . .

FROM: LaytonG@darksidemusictracks.com

TO: Charleston_Richards@BubblePOP.com

Hey, Charli! Hope you made it to LA safely. I assume you're taking a car to the premiere. I'll be there by five, so I should be there when you get there. I need to sit somewhere near the front for the presentation, but if you save me a seat, I'll move back with you for the movie?

Only if you want. I know you're working.

Oh, check this out. Look at these bloopers from taping today. Check out the actor who gets seriously messed up.

—Lay

Inserted at the bottom of the message was a video where the guy who plays a superhero gets jacked up trying to run down a set of stairs, clipping his shoulder on the wall and tumbling the rest of the way down.

He laughed like a hyena, though, so I guessed he didn't mind or get hurt.

I was laughing and smiling too until I realized everyone in the spa was staring at me. Embarrassed, I sobered quickly and shoved my phone back in my purse, and pretended to be fascinated with the color of my toes.

Eight

Layton

"Thanks, Tony," I called out to my tailor.

"No problem, Layton. Knock 'em dead tonight. Especially this young lady," he said, clucking his tongue.

I felt a blush creep up my cheeks like a college girl in love and immediately thought about worms and dirt. When my skin cooled, I turned around.

"Nah, she's just a friend, but it'll be nice to see her." I didn't voice out loud my next thought. *It's been an ongoing fantasy.*

"Yeah, yeah, yeah." Tony shooed me out with his hand into the bright California sunlight.

I shoved my Aviators on my face and headed toward my car. I needed a shower and to ditch the track pants for my tux. I hadn't worn my penguin suit since the last awards show I attended, and it had desperately needed a little adjustment here and there, if you know what I mean.

Earlier in the week, I'd braved the smirky salespeople and ran into Neiman Marcus to buy a new pair of loafers for this occasion and a crisp white shirt.

I was skipping all the other accessories; they just seemed to accentuate my shape—or lack thereof.

Once I got in my car, I cranked the AC and checked my phone. I'd sent Charli my phone number earlier in the week, but hardly expected her to use it.

She's not here for you. She's coming for work. It's a coincidence.

I couldn't help but whip off a quick e-mail. Corresponding with her had become my favorite pastime, an addiction I wasn't willing to admit to having. I knew exactly what I wanted to send her—I'd been sending her funny outtakes all week from filming. She always wrote back the funniest comments like, "Even I could do that stunt without getting injured." Our banter had turned into my favorite part of the day, and some days, I imagined it was hers too.

After I hurt her feelings on the plane, it became a bit of a compulsion to try to make her smile. Flowers were one thing . . . now I was going to see her face-to-face.

I didn't expect much. Certainly nothing like my fantasies.

Maybe she was a personality girl?

I had that in spades.

Or she loved the strong, gentlemanly type?

I worked that too.

Whatever she wants, I'll be, I chanted to myself as I stepped into the shower.

After scrubbing myself clean, I made sure to take care of things down below. No one liked an early blower.

Shut up, Layton. Nothing like that is going to happen tonight.

Well, I was ready in case we did get beyond talking this evening.

Although it didn't matter. The promise of an evening with Charli was enough to satisfy a guy like me.

Nine

Charli

I smoothed my hand over my dress, checking for any last-minute creases or lint, and took a long, deep breath.

Crap. I covered fitness, not Hollywood, yet here I was, sweating like a pig in the backseat of a limo. There was a good reason I was a health-and-fitness editor and not a paparazzi gal. I preferred running shorts to ball gowns.

Dressing up made me nervous. It meant small talk and cocktails with people who always questioned my age and position. Everything was subjective.

With writing and editing, there were rules for grammar and punctuation. With running and spinning, there were times finished, pace, calories burned, heart rate.

Numbers don't lie.

The car made its approach to the theater and slowed before a red carpet spread out long and wide, filled with celebrities and surrounded by the media. Strobe lights lit the place up against the dusky sky. When the limo stilled, I breathed in through my nose and out through my mouth once and then again before the driver opened my door. It was just another weekday here in Westwood—at least that's what I told myself.

I stepped out and felt bare as all eyes focused on me until they realized I was no one, and then they all went back to the hot guy they were ogling before, all fit and tan with a man bun and a beard.

Thankful for the distraction, I quickly made my way past the paps and into the theater. A woman in a long black evening gown asked for my name.

"Charli Richards."

She ran a finger down the list on her sparkly clipboard, and when she scrunched her face, I added, "From *BubblePOP*."

"Charleston?"

"Yes, that's me."

"Welcome to *Seven Sins of Serial Dating*. Both lounges are open inside, and you may bring your drinks into the theater."

"Thank you."

As I took a moment to take in my surroundings, I decided a glass of wine was in order. I politely pushed my way close to the bar and waited for a server.

"Can I help you?"

"White wine spritzer, please."

The bartender turned around and grabbed a bottle of white wine and a chilled glass. When he turned back around with my drink, a hand came out of nowhere and took the glass from him.

"Hey there, gorgeous girl." Layton handed me my beverage, massaging my body with his voice. He shoved a five-dollar bill into a glass for tips and turned back to me. "You made it."

His eyes seared through me, as warm and genuine as they had been on the plane. I took a sip of my drink and swallowed any weird thoughts I'd been having.

"Here I am. God, this is something. Makes covering the New York Half Marathon feel like nothing."

"Welcome to the land of make-believe."

"So, were you waiting for me?" I took a look around; he seemed to come out of nowhere.

Double crap, why did I have to go and get bitchy again?

"I guess," he said. "I asked for them to give me a buzz when you arrived. Hope that's okay?"

I nodded and smiled for fear that the words *a bit stalkerish, but I like it*, or even worse, *I'm so glad you did*, would come out of my mouth.

"Uh-oh." He stuck his hand inside his pocket and pulled out a rosebud, tight and not quite ready to bloom. "For you." His long fingers extended the deep purple flower toward me. "Want to hold it? Or you can pin it? They gave me a pin . . ."

"It's beautiful," I said, twisting it in my manicured fingers. I popped it into the snap on my clutch. "I think it looks stunning here. Does that work?"

"If it's good for you, it's good for me." He winked and I took notice of his hair, styled and handsome in a way only a few men could pull off.

"You look great," he added. "Definitely, the most gorgeous woman here." His eyes ran the length of my red dress, not stopping when it ended above my knees.

"Thanks. You clean up well yourself." Taking in his tux and Italian loafers, I decided he didn't look half-bad. The penguin suit was way better than the Beastie Boys tee . . . or maybe not?

What is it about this guy? On paper, he's one hundred percent wrong for me. His e-mails are equal parts annoying and funny.

Okay, more funny than annoying. More like refreshing. Different. Exciting.

But as I stand next to him now, he's giving me head-to-toe tingles, and I find myself dwelling on his e-mails.

"Thanks. To answer your question, I asked them to grab me when you got here because I was afraid we wouldn't connect. I have to go backstage, but do you want to grab something to eat after this? I mean, you flew all the way here, and I thought I could show you around."

He was obviously rambling, and ran a now visibly shaky hand through his styled hair before smoothing it back into place. To me, he looked better with it mussed.

I commanded my eyes to move from his hair and meet his gaze, and then almost wished I hadn't. There was something about his eyes. They were compelling. Alluring.

"Sounds good," I said, flattered he gave them my name and nervous about him asking me to dinner.

"Let's meet here when it's over? This way you don't have to hold a seat for me during the movie and you can actually enjoy the film, and I'm not interrupting with all my fun facts, if that's cool with you? I just want you to have a good time."

He was rambling again, and all I wanted to do was run my fingers through his hair and fluff it.

"That sounds good. Since I have to report on this movie, I should concentrate."

"So, I'll see you back here."

"Yes, right here," I said, nodding. It felt as though we both needed the confirmation.

As we stood there for a beat and then one more, I wasn't sure what to do. We'd made a plan, and it was unclear what he was waiting for . . . but then he leaned in and kissed me on the cheek.

Oh, that's what he waited for!

His lips lingered a bit too long for it to be a brotherly or cousinly kiss, but it wasn't on the lips. Instead, his mouth caressed my cheek. I sensed a whisper of doubt on his part—*should he be doing this?*—along with a heavy dose of want, as if he'd been waiting a long time to do it.

Confusion and need clouded my own thoughts like the smog had clouded the air when I landed this morning.

My phone provided a welcome distraction when it buzzed in my clutch as Layton made his way back to wherever he needed to be. I pulled it out, punched in my code, and read my text.

Janie: Send me pics of the hotties! TAKE ONE HOME! Sorry. I didn't mean to scream in ALL CAPS . . . yes, I DID! Take one home.

Funny, I hadn't even noticed any hotties, let alone one I wanted to take home.

The movie was actually great. It was witty and sappy, sweet and sassy, funny and sentimental; basically everything you want in a rom-com. I took my time leaving the theater, eavesdropping on all the unofficial reviews and making some mental notes about the audience's favorite scenes as I made my way to our meeting spot.

It didn't help that my starved stomach rumbled. It was past my bedtime at home, and I hadn't eaten much during the day because of the slinky red dress I was wearing and the lack of Spanx.

I found a spot near the bar and typed a couple of notes into my phone.

The scene where she drops her scarf in the grate and bends over to pick it up, about to give the whole city a peep show, and the hero quickly comes up and hides her bare ass, hugging her from behind.

The restaurant scene where they share garlic bread and make a point of kissing as soon as they leave the table, commingling garlicky breath.

Don't forget to mention the sound track. The music was spot-on . . . in fact, would make a great playlist for a long run.

"Eeep!" I jumped a foot in the air when I felt a hand on my shoulder.

"Oh, wow, I'm sorry. I didn't mean to scare you. Shit." Layton berated himself, closing his eyes tightly and cursing.

"No worries. I was making some notes for the review and I was concentrating. You scared the heck out of me."

His cheeks deepened in color. "Not quite the reaction I was going for."

"Well, I won't forget it," I teased him, letting him off the hook. Obviously, I'd checked my bitchy self away, and I can't say I was upset about it.

Ten

Layton

When I first saw Charli standing there in her red dress, my tongue nearly rolled out of my mouth like Roger Rabbit. In my head I heard, *You're so far out of your league, Lay*, but my feet had a mind of their own. Stepping quickly and confidently toward the bar, I was inches from her almost bare back in seconds. I gulped down my fears and insecurities, my pride, and every negative thought about myself, and snatched her wineglass from the bartender.

She turned quickly, obviously ready to lay into whoever stole her cocktail until she saw me. I'm not going to lie—when her eyes met mine, my heart quickened and my dick hardened. Not just a little stiffy. I was as hard as a fucking light saber, or sword, or whatever . . . a rod.

And there was nothing little about my dick. It was a very pleasing one, or so a few women have told me. Pair it with my smile and I was considered deadly in some circles.

Hey, dorks need lovers too! I might be chunky and quirky, but I'd had my share of women.

But this woman was nothing like the women I'd had before, and I didn't have a clue what to do with her. My fingers burned and itched to touch her. Anywhere. Even a small touch on her shoulder set my insides ablaze. She was petite, confident, smart, savvy, and sexy as all get-out, and my body raged in a way I'd never experienced. My brain and body soaked her in; my blood raced to get closer.

She was also covered in a cloak of insecurity—something I had little to no experience with in women. Geeky women were surprisingly confident in their likes and dislikes. Charli gave off a fascinating vibe. Gorgeous on the outside, jumbled on the inside.

Would she like a commanding touch? A gentle one?

My words lodged in my throat and I considered running to the restroom, rubbing one out and splashing cold water on my face. Instead, I rambled.

I'd quickly deduced there was no way I could sit next to this girl in the movie without my dick bursting through my tuxedo pants—which were tight as it was. Luckily, I had a small amount of brain still functioning and decided to let her work during the movie and steal her for dinner afterward.

Now here she was, all toned and trim, the red dress doing little to conceal how fit she was, and I'd gone and scared the living hell out of her.

Good going, Lay.

"I loved the movie," she said, letting me off the hook. "In fact, look here. I made a note of how good the sound track was."

"Oh, you don't have to say that." I blushed harder than I ever had before. It was becoming a really bad habit when I was around Charli.

"It was really awesome."

Her smile lit up her face. It was the first time I'd seen her do that, and I hoped she did it regularly from my e-mails. She had perfectly white teeth behind red-painted lips. It was fucking sexy.

"So freaking creative to mix up rock and pop in the same sound track."

"Yeah?"

"It sounded cool, the gruff voice against the sugary-sweet beat. I liked it a lot."

"Thanks. Are you hungry?" I changed the subject mostly because I couldn't handle the compliment from her. It made me want to march around the room, pounding my chest and yelling, *She likes me! My music. Me. Me. Me.*

"Starved. I hope it's okay to admit that here in the land of pretty people. Though, I'm not sure I'd ever say that at home either."

The last part trailed off as if she was talking to herself, mumbling the truth, trying to convince herself to get out of Dodge. Her gaze traveled to the floor, her eyes half fluttering in quick embarrassment at her words.

After all, I wasn't exactly pretty.

"What are you in the mood for?" I completely ignored her fumble, hoping it was the right move.

"Sushi? Do you like it?"

"I know just the place," I lied.

I'd never been there. I'd wanted to go, but it was a hot, trendy spot. Definitely not the type of place I'd hit up with the guys. Plus, sushi never quite satisfied me. But with Charli, I was already full.

Christ, I'm turning into a romantic cornball.

"Great!"

"I brought my car. Would you like to ride with me?" I didn't know what the protocol was. She'd clearly taken a car service to the premiere, and she was an independent New York City girl—woman.

"Sure." She swallowed and her delicate pink tongue came out to swipe over her red lips. "You're not going to steal me and sell me off to Mexico or anything?"

"They do like blondes down there."

Somewhere I found the confidence to snatch her hand in mine and squeeze it. I winked as I joked and she laughed, her giggle filling the air all around us. I wanted to reach out and grab it, shove it in my pocket, and save it for a bad day.

"You're funny, Layton G."

"Glad you think so, Charli. Come on."

I led her toward the exit and out into the crisp nighttime air, handed the valet my ticket, and turned toward my . . . date? Friend? Acquaintance?

"Cold?" I asked.

She was running her hands up and down her arms. I watched tiny goose bumps pop out on her creamy skin like it was an Oscar-winning movie.

"Here." I shrugged off my jacket and wrapped it over her shoulders. It engulfed her in a way that was almost comical.

"I thought it would be warmer," she admitted, pulling the jacket tighter around her. "Thanks."

My car drove up, and the valet jumped out of the driver's side and opened the passenger door for Charli. Of course, he did.

She handed me my jacket and slid into the black leather seat of my BMW, the skirt of her dress riding up her leg. I tucked my tongue back into my mouth for the second time this evening.

"Drive safely," the valet called out, never taking his eyes off my passenger.

I turned the key and looked toward Charli, noting the small wisps of her blond hair framing her face. "Ready?"

She nodded, a slight smile settling on her lips as she set her hands in her lap and looked toward the city in front of us.

Pulling out into traffic, I hit the button on the steering wheel to turn on the stereo. Ed Sheeran flooded the car. Hey, I worked in music . . . I knew which tunes got the ladies comfortable.

"Truth is, I've never been to this place but I've wanted to go," I said, starting to ramble again. What I didn't mention was that afterward, I'd probably hit up the In-and-Out so I wouldn't go to bed hungry.

"I'm excited to eat anywhere. I had to starve myself all day to fit in this dress—" She stopped short and covered her mouth with her hand.

Me too, except it was a tux and not a dress, I wanted to admit, but I didn't.

"Sorry," she said with an embarrassed grin. "That was TMI, but it's true."

"Well, they keep mentioning Zao's in the LA mag, and it even had a quick write-up in Esquire last month. It's not far, which is also a bonus because everything out here is a pain in the ass."

"Where do you live? Near here?"

"I'm over in Santa Monica, maybe twenty, thirty minutes with light traffic. It's a pretty cool neighborhood, hip, whatever. I bought a run-down bungalow on a jumbo mortgage when I started my biz. It was a bit of a gamble, but I needed the space for my own studio, and it was cheaper than renting one. So I put one in, and it's paid off. And you? Back east?"

"I live in the Meatpacking District. An old warehouse converted into condos. I live by myself . . . I actually don't do well with roommates."

"Really?"

"I'm a bit intolerant of others when I'm working or getting ready for a run. I don't know; I just like my own space." She ran a finger behind her ear, securing her hair behind it, and turned her gaze out the passenger window.

"I get it. Actually, I don't do that well living with others either. In college after the first year, I opted for a single."

She smiled again; I could see the corner of her mouth raise in profile, and it was brilliant. "I was always the odd one left out in college because I was so far ahead, but younger without an ID. Maybe that's why I never really got into roommates. I was always left behind. Until I met Janie. She's my closest friend back home."

"I still hang with a few of my buddies from school. We were all kind of a bit off-beat—" I said, then stopped short as anxiety got the better of me. "I don't know why I'm saying all this shit. I'm a bit nervous, to be honest."

"Why?"

"It's not every night I have a stunning, intelligent woman in my car. Let alone one who looks as good as you do in that dress."

I let it all hang out there. After all, I'd corresponded for weeks via e-mail with Charli. If she didn't know by now I had a crush on her, I clearly wasn't doing anything right.

She gave me a polite smile. "We barely know each other, so there's no reason to be nervous. You're just being a welcoming host to me. It's not like you have to impress me."

And there you have it. She didn't know I was into her, or else didn't want to admit it to herself. I had failed.

Just then, we pulled up to Zao's, and another valet ran to open her door and openly gawked as she exited the car. His eyes ran her full length, pausing at her sexy-as-fuck shoes before making their way back up to her cleavage. Good thing she didn't seem to notice.

This time, I didn't grab her hand. We walked into the restaurant side by side after the overeager valet grabbed the door.

"Heyyy, welcome to Zao's. Do you have a reservation?" The hostess was nearly toppling over in her five-inch heels and the sausage skin masquerading as a black dress.

Fuck. Reservations.

The place thumped and bumped all around us thanks to the live DJ in the corner, who clearly didn't know how to adjust the bass.

"You know what? Bernie Ross from production was supposed to call ahead for me. I'm Layton Griffin . . . I'm one of the sound guys over at MGM." I acted quickly, thought up something like a dog in heat, desperate to get knocked up. I would never have this chance again.

"Bernie? Let me look." She ran her gaze up and down the iPad in front of her, tapping open apps with her finger. "Shell, did someone from Bernie Ross's place a call?"

Who knew Bernie was such a bigwig here?

A woman's disembodied voice came from the iPad; apparently it doubled as their phone as well. "Who knows? If he's with Bernie, give him a table by the window."

The hostess stared at me for less than a beat before she grabbed a couple of iPads that obviously doubled as menus and said, "This way."

Wow, it worked!

My fingers grazed Charli's back, urging her to go in front of me, and instantly caught fire. And really, I wasn't so hard up, but the light touch was magnetic.

The hostess led us toward a two-top against the window. I scurried ahead to beat her at pulling out a chair for Charli, ignoring the awkwardness of the hostess trying to wedge herself around me as Charli paused and witnessed the whole thing.

It was better than watching the *Return of the Jedi* when Charli turned on her iPad. Her features were softly illuminated by the glow, emphasizing her plump and tender lips, as her gaze focused on the backlit menu in front of her.

"Do you like the raw stuff?" Charli's question brought me out of my trance.

"Yeah. I pretty much like everything."

And would need a few slices of pizza later . . . my usual sushi routine.

The server came over and welcomed us with more pomp and circumstance than I thought was usual. The Bernie factor, I assumed.

We ordered a few rolls and some sashimi. Charli ordered a glass of prosecco; I opted for a Sapporo. Mostly, we made small talk about the movie while we waited for the drinks.

"Cheers to first class and my lucky seat . . . 2D." I touched my cold can to her glass.

"Ha," she said, taking a sip of her sparkling drink.

Her blond hair contrasted sharply against the black walls, so shiny under the overhead lights of the restaurant. I wanted to run my fingers through it.

"So, New York all the time. That must be intense?" I focused on her collarbone and shoulders for a moment. They were perfect, slight, but not too bony. I'd give my left nut to be with a woman like this.

"It's home. I'm used to it, been there since right after college. I have a routine, and I work a lot. Although, this place is pretty crazy itself."

"It is, but out here everyone's in the 'business' and we all drive around in our cars and show up fashionably late. Well, not me always. I'm a behind-the-scenes guy, and I guess I like fading into the background like that, especially in a town like this, where it's all so plastic." There I went again with my tell-all, diarrhea mouth.

"It does feel a bit fake out here, like everything's so perfect. But I'm sure New York seems that way to some people."

"I had a good time there, but I couldn't believe how people rush around. I never can, anytime I'm there. I like being behind my mixing table with my headphones in my studio."

Her eyes crinkled the tiniest bit at my comment. For some reason, she got my need to have space. Although, I doubted that she and I shared that quirk for the same reasons.

I was an outcast, and Charli? Well, she was a perfectionist.

But also perfect to the human eye.

Eleven

Charli

Hot and flushed, I finished my prosecco a lot faster than normal. This guy listened to Ed Sheeran, drove a BMW, and was totally . . . unexpected.

Then again, I wasn't sure what I expected. Perhaps a man conjured up from Janie's expectations and my mom's recent fixations?

I did come partly for him, expecting him to make me laugh, but this? The whole thing with him being a romantic James Dean crossed with John Cusack, *that* I wasn't prepared for. *Except for his build.*

Of course, he'd cleaned up well for tonight. His black hair was parted and styled, gelled into place. His teeth were white, and a light wave of cologne wafted from him. His tux was a tad tight, his stomach not entirely constrained by the pants, but from the shoulders up, he was a looker.

God, Charleston . . . get a grip.

But I was having a lot of fun, more fun than I should be having. This was a work trip, and it was only a convenient coincidence that Layton was here with me at dinner. *Right?*

"I'm sure your studio is cool," I said. "I think when you love what you do, that's all that matters."

His brow furrowed and his eyes locked on mine. Silver flecks sparked in his irises when he went in for the kill. "Do you like what you do?"

Automatically, my hand went for my empty champagne glass.

"Would you like another?" His gaze drifted around the restaurant, looking for a server.

"I'd better not. I barely ate today." Inside my head, my brain was wildly waving a red flag. I was enjoying myself entirely too much, and there was no need for more booze.

"Do you like what you do?" Layton obviously wasn't going to let it go. He was too perceptive for that.

"I do, but I liked writing more. Now I spend my days axing ideas and cutting copy. I sort of want a change already, but it feels wrong. I'm only twenty-eight. Too young for this kind of crisis."

Layton's hand found its way on top of mine. "Hey, it's never too early or late to want changes."

I couldn't take my gaze off his hand covering mine. He had long fingers with small calluses that tickled my skin, and his palm was warm.

He caught my gaze locked on the sight. "Oh, sorry. God, I didn't mean to overstep my boundaries."

"It's okay."

When he pulled his hand back quickly, my fingers felt cold. The absence of his warm palm left me hungry for more of him. For *him*!

This guy, Layton Griffin—enigmatic introvert, chunky monkey, resident funny guy, and apparently a Casanova—scared the shit out of me. There was no polite, educated, ladylike way of putting it.

"Excuse me, I have to use the ladies' room."

Layton stood while I lumbered out of my chair, tripping over my own two feet, rushing to get away from the unfamiliar sensations I was feeling.

In the bathroom, I stared at my reflection in the mirror—the few wispy layers of my blond hair framing my face, the lipstick smeared off my top lip, the tiny speck of mascara under my eye, and the heart beating wildly in my chest. It was racing so hard, I could see it pounding against my skin.

I closed my eyes and took big gulps of air, inhaling deep breaths and exhaling them with a whoosh, trying desperately to calm myself.

Stalling, I peed, washed my hands, and pulled out my phone to text Janie.

Charli: SOS. Please text or call shortly and say you need me. Bad breakup, death in the family, whatever you want. Need out of a dinner. Please.

I jammed the phone back in my small purse and made my way back to the table. Of course, Layton stood again as I approached, and had also waited for me to come back before eating. The food had arrived and was displayed around the table.

"Good thing none of it's hot," he teased.

"Looks amazing," I said, and picked up my chopsticks to place a few rolls and pieces of sashimi on my plate.

"I guess we're not at that stage in our relationship where we can just pluck off the serving dish. Not that we're in any kind of relationship . . . I just meant, you go ahead and take what you want."

Layton's cheeks pinked as he stumbled over his words, and the sight of it made my heart thump a rapid pace again. I'd never made anyone nervous before.

Was it flattering? Or was it a turnoff?

I moaned over a piece of salmon, my stomach thanking me for some food. I left the rice and moved on to the tuna.

"It's good, really good. I was starving," I said to fill in the silence.

Layton had busied himself with a shrimp tempura roll. At my comment, he looked up and nodded.

"It's living up to all the hype. This spicy sauce is the bomb," he said after swallowing.

"Why have you never been here? I'd be here all the time if I lived here."

The back of my neck was beginning to feel damp. I didn't know if it was nerves or excitement or both. Where the heck was Janie?

"I don't know. Like I said, I've heard of it. It's the hot place right now, but I usually do sushi takeout near my house . . . and then pizza delivery," Layton said with a stilted laugh.

"Really?" I chuckled politely, but really? Is that what he did?

"I guess I shouldn't admit to it."

"I'm sure a lot of people do it."

"You don't." He raised an eyebrow.

"Well no, but I'm not a big eater."

Geez, this whole conversation and evening just took a bad turn. What the hell did I know? Men probably couldn't survive on sushi alone.

"And you're a fitness editor, so pizza is probably a no-no." He tried to say it lightly, to make it a joke, but his words came out tense.

"I like pizza . . . on special occasions."

Layton laughed, and it felt like it was directed at himself. My heart sank.

"Hey, it's no biggie. And you went out of your way to show me LA, so let's not ruin this evening."

My heart broke for this guy. Everyone probably judged him the way I first did when I sat in seat 2C, and here I was doing it all over again.

Just then, my purse began buzzing on the table. *Janie.*

Huh. I wasn't sure I wanted her to rescue me anymore. I held up a finger to Layton, signaling him to give me a sec.

After digging my phone from my purse, I swiped a finger over the screen and turned my head to the side. "Hello?"

"Oh, thank God, Char, you're there! Poppy died! Waaahhh," Janie screamed through the phone, loud enough that the whole restaurant probably heard.

"Slow down, Janie." We had a well-oiled routine when it came to bad-date rescues. It was always Poppy or Nana and included a lot of tears.

"Popppy diiied," she wailed, sounding convincingly pitiful.

"I'm in LA, sweetie, but I can take the red-eye home . . ."

Her wails turned to stuttering sobs. "R-r-really?"

Layton stared at me. His hair had fallen a bit on his forehead, and he pushed it back so he could give me his full attention.

"Hold on one sec, Janie," I said into the phone and twisted my body back toward Layton. Cupping my hand over the microphone, I spoke to him in a hushed tone. "My friend's grandfather died. Janie, the one I told you about. I have to go."

He nodded, his face stoic.

Disappointment flooded every inch of my body. This was what I had wanted, to get out of this evening, and now he was letting me go without a protest.

"Janie, I'll text you when I know my plans. Take a warm shower and relax," I said soothingly into the phone and disconnected the call.

"Too bad," Layton said, his face still expressionless.

My belly ached from a weird hunger—and not for food.

"I'm so sorry. I can't leave her waiting." I pulled out my clutch and started to take out my company card.

"Hey, it's on me. I'll get the bill and take you where you need to go."

His left eye twitched the slightest bit, and if he wasn't such a large and looming presence, I would have thought he was holding back tears. That wasn't his style, though. He was too proud.

"You know what? Is it okay if I grab an Uber or a cab? I hate to send you out of your way, and I really have to go."

If this wasn't what I wanted, then why was I running the hell out of there?

Because this wasn't me. This guy—the closeness, the intimate conversation—none of it was me. Even if it felt amazing, like stoking a fire on a cold night, I wasn't meant for this. I had a plan and I was sticking to it. Big city, even bigger dreams, and a huge life were in my future.

"It's not out of my way—"

"It wouldn't sit well with me. This has been great. I loved the movie. Thanks, Layton."

I stood and so did he. We stood there in an uncomfortable silence for a beat as my mind raced, my uncertainty lingering.

I might be a successful woman but I was acting like a middle school girl, ditching a boy at the arcade. And of course, I ran.

Because that's what I do.

Layton made the first move, leaned in and kissed my cheek. This time, he didn't linger. It was a chaste brush of his lips, and more than disappointment flooded my veins. Shame, self-loathing, and vile thoughts wound their way through my soul.

But I had to follow through because this was so messed up.

"'Bye, Layton. Thank you."

I rushed out into the night where a small line of cab drivers waited across the street.

Twelve

Layton

Spread out on my bed, flat on my back, my shirt wrinkled and untucked, I stared at the ceiling. "That was a bust," I said to no one.

I closed my eyes tight and let out a deep sigh. Even though I'd done enough rom-coms and dramedy films to know the phone call was bullshit, a small sliver of me wished differently but I knew.

Was I that gross? I'd even tried to tighten up the last week. Instead of tossing the ball to Harriette on the beach, I actually walked her every morning. I thought I'd cleaned up okay and had actually been hopeful of getting the girl.

Right, not only a girl. I could do that; I was funny and full of wit. But this was *the* girl, the one worth chasing, the one worth going all out for.

And then she'd practically run the hell out of the restaurant, even taking a cab, happy to let some other nobody drive her back to the hotel and to the airport.

My phone buzzed in my back pocket. For a fleeting moment, I was hopeful once again, but the screen read PETER. No such luck for my renewed hope.

"What's up?" I sat up and answered the phone, but when I caught a glance of myself in the mirror, I plopped back down.

"You done with your fancy gig?"

I hadn't mentioned my cyber-affair with Charli at all to my friends. It was less about being embarrassed and more about not wanting to share the few moments of happiness we had. Or I had.

"Yeah, I'm home." I kicked off my loafers and heard each one make a low thud on the hardwood floor.

"A bunch of us are down at Bastion's. Come on down."

Harriette clicked through the room and jumped up on the bed next to me, shoving her face in mine. I guess I wasn't alone. If golden retrievers count.

"I'm fucking tired. I don't know."

"Come on, Griff, don't be a twat-waffle. We're ordering wings, so get your fat ass down here. Plus, we're gonna hustle some dudes in pool and we need a big guy."

Peter was a stand-up comic, or waiter, depending on the day. He thought he was funny, but I wasn't so sure.

"Fine, fine. I got to change and I'll be around. Don't get into any bar fights."

He disconnected without a word, and I rolled off my bed and headed toward my closet. I peeled off my tux and threw it into a ball in the corner. I'd probably skip the next premiere, anyway. Opting for a worn-in pair of jeans and a flannel thrown over a Stones T-shirt, I shoved my feet into a pair of Chucks.

"Come on, girl," I called to Harriette, and let her into the backyard for a quick pee.

She did her thing, I gave her a cookie, and I walked up the street to the main drag toward Bastion's. It was a trendy bar with all the old-school fun stuff like pool and darts.

A small crowd of people stood so many feet away from the door smoking, and I brushed past them and into the bar. It was dim with a DJ spinning tunes in the corner.

I decided to stop at the bar first . . . I needed something to erase the earlier events.

"Whiskey, make it a double," I shouted across the glass bar.

Lots of pretty people occupied the stools, laughing and clinking their glasses without a care in the world. Women with long, shiny hair and men in fitted Henleys and skinny jeans.

I was invisible to them.

I grabbed my drink and tossed back half, the burn making me forget the few minutes I wasn't invisible—the half hour when Charli looked at me, not through me or around me. As soon as I removed the glass from my lips, the moment was over.

I threw some money on the bar and made my way to the back, finishing my drink by the time I made it to the pool table.

"Griff! What's happening, man? You ditch the penguin suit?" Peter greeted me over his pool cue before bending over the table to take a shot.

"Hey, Griff." Adam slapped me on the back and silently motioned toward the bucket of beer. "So, the super-famous Katie didn't drag you back home?" the ass had the balls to ask me as I grabbed a bottle of Heineken.

"I'm her Saturday-night man."

"You wish," he tossed back.

"Actually, she's not the girl for me." The whiskey was now having an unexpected effect. Rather than calming me, it was acting like a truth serum.

"Oh yeah." Peter looked up. "You'd throw her out of bed, I'm sure."

I took a big swig of my beer and looked toward him, taking in his scrawny frame, wire-rim glasses, and unkempt brown hair. "She may prefer you, big guy!"

He ran a hand through his hair and jutted his hip out. "You know what, you may be right." He proceeded to sashay around the table as if I'd said he thought he was funny.

"I got next," I hollered and settled onto a stool to wait. "Who the hell are you playing, anyway?"

"I'm warming up, letting my shooting arm get ready."

"This isn't basketball, Pete. You know that, right?"

He ignored me.

"Can I get you guys anything?"

A scantily clad waitress with long red hair sidled up next to Adam. He was the good-looking one of our gang. By day, he was a lawyer at one of the studios, and by night he was our resident manwhore.

His words, not mine. Seriously.

"Wings, mild with bleu cheese, coupla orders, doll," Peter yelled.

The ginger glared at him.

"Ignore him, honey." Adam stood close to her, running a hand through his shaggy blond hair as he winked at her. "We'll have some wings, please, and how about another bucket of beers?"

"Anything for you," she said, swinging her hips from side to side as she headed back to the kitchen.

"Guess who's going home with her tonight?" Adam asked us, then turned both of his thumbs toward his cashmere-clad chest and declared, "This dude."

His eyes damn near sparkled at the prospect, and I wondered what it felt like to have women be such an easy conquest for you.

Once the waitress was out of sight, Adam turned his gaze back on me. "So, if a Hollywood superstar isn't enough for you, does that mean you met someone else? A better woman?"

"Nah. Thought I might have, but nope."

"Interesting. I notice your hair's all styled. Was she there tonight?"

"Adam, what are we . . . two girls trading secrets over coffee? Shut the fuck up and get ready to play pool. Hopefully the funny guy is almost warmed up."

He held his palms up in the air in mock surrender. "Okay, tough guy. Don't shoot me for asking."

"Didn't you hear me? Shut the fuck up."

I didn't need any crap from Mr. Wonderful. All I wanted to do was eat some wings (because I was still hungry), play pool, and forget about earlier.

I wasn't having much success, though. The reel of Charli running out on me was stuck on replay in my head.

Thirteen

Charli

Like a fool, I hid in my hotel room after running out of the restaurant. I had to order room service because as it turned out, sushi wasn't filling.

The next morning, I took the first flight out, rushing back to the Big Apple as if something incredible was waiting for me. In fact, nothing but work was waiting.

The premiere was on a Thursday and I was originally scheduled to stay in California until Saturday, so when I slipped back into the office late Friday afternoon, I was greeted by a lot of raised eyebrows.

I didn't let it bother me. Grabbing my messages and the proofs waiting for me on my desk, I turned right around and headed home for a lonely weekend, intending to fill it with work and exercise.

When I got home that night and checked my messages like I usually do, I had an e-mail from him.

FROM: LaytonG@darksidemusictracks.com
TO: Charleston_Richards@BubblePOP.com

SUBJECT: Did you get home safely?

Charli –

I want to believe it was merely bad luck our evening was interrupted. Either way, I wanted to make sure you got back home safely.

Can't wait to read your review of the movie.

—Layton

P.S. Look what my dog did to my tuxedo loafers.

Attached was a picture of a big, fuzzy golden retriever holding a half-chewed Ferragamo loafer in his or her mouth.

I didn't even know Layton had a dog. How could this mean anything between us if I didn't know something like that?

Well, for starters, you didn't even give him a chance to say he had a dog.

Janie had wanted to hang out that night, but I refused. Instead, I worked out and ate a quick dinner, then went through the rest of my work e-mails.

For the rest of the weekend, I ran myself ragged, collapsing into bed each evening, crossing my fingers I was exhausted enough to ignore the e-mail sitting so innocently in my in-box.

The one I didn't respond to.

Either way, I wanted to make sure you got back home safely.

That sentence played on repeat in my head, plaguing me for five days until I finally gave in. By Tuesday, I couldn't outrun or outspin my demons anymore.

FROM: Charleston_Richards@BubblePOP.com

TO: LaytonG@darksidemusictracks.com

SUBJECT: ~~I'm back. Thanks.~~ Thank you

~~Thank you so much for your concern.~~

Thanks for asking. I did get home in one piece, and have been swamped with deadlines.

It's been raining here all week and I miss the LA sun, but it's good for my workload.

Fondly,

Charli

P.S. Hope you made your dog pay for your shoes.

I'd returned to hitting the backspace key more than any other, so I hit SEND before I mentioned anything but the weather or my work, and especially not the reason why I fled.

He knew it was an excuse.

Either way, I wanted to make sure you got back home safely.

He definitely knew. My leaving was the proverbial elephant in the room, a big one growing by the minute.

I went to bed that night without checking my e-mail again—an occupational hazard but an emotional safeguard.

Ever since I got back to New York, when I thought back to our moments in the car or seated at Zao's, I felt myself smiling, my chest warming, and my defense mechanisms melting. There was something about this guy. I liked him, but I shouldn't.

My mind ticked off all the reasons I shouldn't like him as I slipped into a hot bath on Wednesday night, wanting to wash myself of my guilt and maybe relax a little while I was at it.

First, I was a fitness editor in New York City. And Layton . . . well, he was anything but fit.

Second, I had a big career ahead of me, something my mom never did after meeting my dad. Wasn't that why I became so convinced I needed the career first . . . from watching her? Now she'd changed her tune, but I wasn't changing.

Third, I couldn't chase around this earth for a dude, something my mom did for my dad. I hadn't graduated from high school a year early and college three semesters too soon for this . . . to be saddled to the fun-loving guy. When I finally got hitched, it would be to some corporate bigshot, just like Janie said I should.

Wallowing in remorse, I covered my face with my hands, splashing soapy water all over the place.

I'm a bitch. And I'm not even happy being one. I'm allowing my friend to lead me around, telling me what to do.

In the short time I'd known this huggable guy, Layton Griffin, did he ever make me feel like he'd want a woman to sacrifice her dreams for him?

No, but we were certainly nowhere near that stage.

That stupid night. Actually, it was a beautiful night, and I was the stupid one.

"Ugh," I muttered and sank deeper in the water.

When my phone dinged on the side of the tub, I shook my hand free of water and picked it up. It had been a few hours since I'd checked my messages, and I couldn't stand not checking anymore.

My in-box was flooded with work e-mails. Some women's-only marathon was coming to Central Park, and the magazine was going to be a sponsor. Larissa knew I was close with Janie, and of course, she wanted me to ask the Royal to put us all up for the event, plus a few contest winners. I hated when she made me do that—I was a writer, not a concierge—but this was New York and it was all about who you knew.

There were a few more e-mails, all regarding July's posts, which were already almost filled. We had two more spotlights open, and the pit of writers under me were all clawing to get a feature. So-and-so wanted to interview Katie on her fitness routine. *No to that . . . nothing to do with Katie.*

Another writer wanted to do a feature on dangerous hikes in Colorado.

Could be interesting, but would he travel or only do research?

And of course, Layton replied.

What the heck? I squinted and read the subject twice.

FROM: LaytonG@darksidemusictracks.com

TO: Charleston_Richards@BubblePOP.com

SUBJECT: Harriette is getting a job

Charli –

Glad you got back to me. I was beginning to wonder if you'd been sold to Mexico.

Weather has been nice here, but the smog gets to you after a while, so don't be too envious.

And yes, Harriette—my golden—is scouring LA for temp work to reimburse me for my shoes. In the meantime, she's working her way through a few bones.

She's a good girl, for the most part. Not much of a guard dog and a bit mouthy, but she's dependable.

—Layton

There was no PS or funny video, not even a "Lay" for his signature.

Deciding I'd successfully blown off the guy, I sank deeper in shame and the tub.

Although I didn't feel one bit relaxed.

Fourteen

At the crack of dawn, I climbed onto a spinning bike at the gym, connected my heart-rate monitor, and went the fuck after it. My legs spun as if my life depended on it.

Actually, my sanity did. I was going out of my mind with regret and self-loathing. My only peace came when I was dripping sweat and physically exhausted. My normal once-a-day exercise routine turned out to be completely unsatisfying in the week since I returned from LA, and I'd upped the ante in response.

By the time I exited the spin studio, I was soaked to the bone and dreading the coming weekend. At least I had today at work to keep my schizophrenic mind occupied. I ran home, showered, and took a cab to work. As I took the elevator upstairs, my phone beeped.

Janie: Drinks tonight. No excuses. See you at the Royal, Craig's buying. 6:30.

I didn't even answer. Tonight was Friday, the night Janie and I always got together. There was no hiding from her anymore.

I plowed my way through the day, wielding my red pen and my disapproval of this or that until almost six o'clock. Then I raided the fashion closet, borrowing an emerald-green blouse and a pair of dark green satin Blahniks as I promised Rivvi, our fashion editor, I'd bring them back in one piece.

Freshly changed, teeth brushed, and perfume spritzed, I made my way to the Royal. I indulged in another cab, my mood already too soured to brave public transportation. Inside the hotel, I made my way to the bar and only smiled when Craig set a giant glass of wine in front of me.

"That kind of week?"

"Oh, Craig, you have no idea."

"Work stuff or boy stuff?" He gave me a boyish grin.

"Me stuff," I answered.

"Want to spill? I'm game if you are, and I'm cool if you're not."

His brown eyes were warm like maple syrup, enticing me to dive in, but I just couldn't go there. I hated myself enough, and if I went into my bitchiness with Craig, I knew he'd never look at me the same.

"I'm just going to marinate my troubles in this wine."

"No problem, babe." He winked and went to the other side of the bar to grab an order.

Click, clack, click. I could hear Janie coming from a mile away.

"Hey there, Char. How you doing, honey?" She squeezed me in a half hug.

"I'm good." I only half smiled.

It was also a night of half truths. I wasn't good or well or even just okay.

"Hey, Craig," Janie called out as she sat down next to me.

"Martini?"

"Yes, sir."

"Now for real, tell me how you are." Janie leaned in close and stared me down.

Her eyes were perfectly lined in black, her lids dusted in glitter, her pink lips were two shades lighter than her blouse, and she smelled like morning dew. I looked at her, really looked at her, preferring to concentrate on her perfections than my imperfections.

"Char," Janie whined, dragging me from my funk.

"I'm okay. Just confused, you know?"

"No, I don't know. Honestly, I've never seen you like this." She downed a gulp of her martini and studied me. "You're always the one so confident and collected. I'm the spaz, but now you're all over the place emotionally."

"I can't explain it. When I met Layton on the plane, I was just . . . so mean. I never considered myself judgmental, but there I was turning my nose up at him and ready to toss him out of first class."

"Char, you're a young, bright, and successful New Yorker. Do you really need to obsess over some slobby music guy?"

My hand shot out and covered her mouth. "Stop! Don't do that. See? That's my exact point. He's a decent guy, went all out of his way to show me a nice evening, and then even worried if I got home when he knew I was bullshitting him." It all came running out of my mouth without a filter or a breath. "And," I stuck my finger in the air, "what do I do? I just shit on him because why?"

"Don't do this," Janie pleaded.

"Because I hate myself. All my life, I rushed through everything—school, internships, jobs—just to get here and I hate it. Freaking despise it."

I guzzled my wine and eyed Craig, who ran over with the bottle and filled me back up, no longer offering to listen to me.

Janie glared at me. "So, get a new job or something, but don't go off the rails because of some guy who means nothing."

"That's just it, J. Why can't he mean something?"

She crooked her finger and signaled for Craig to come back. "Craig, doll, isn't Char a ten? She's got everything, the whole package. Brains, beauty, breasts . . . even with all that running."

I'm a 32B. I hardly call that breasts, but whatever.

"Don't answer that, Craig," I said with a scowl. "Don't feel like you have to lie."

Janie smacked my arm. "Seriously, stop. You do. Nod your head if you agree, Craig."

He nodded like a good puppy and escaped to the other side of the bar. The place was now full of people—sophisticated New Yorkers, yuppies and intellectuals, all pretending to be the city's best.

Blech. But isn't that what I always wanted? What I always did? How I always acted?

"Look around you," Janie said, motioning around the room with her hand. "This is your life, not some big, gentle, introverted music guy."

My stomach churned, bile made its way up my throat, and I had to go.

"You know what? I don't feel so great. I have to go."

I stood and grabbed my purse and jacket. Slipping my arms through the buttery leather, I couldn't help but remember Layton sliding his tux jacket over my shoulders. If I thought hard enough, I could smell him—the rain or dew, the cinnamon and the beer.

Janie stood and tried to wrap me up in her arms. "Charli, I'm sorry. Please don't go."

"Seriously, it's fine. I've just had a long week."

Tossing my bag across my body, I hightailed it out of there.

And went straight home to Lucy.

FROM: Charleston_Richards@BubblePOP.com
TO: LaytonG@darksidemusictracks.com
SUBJECT: God, I'm so sorry

Layton –

I'm so sorry. I'm not even sure why I feel compelled to write this, but I do. There's that and I've had some wine. Okay, a little more than some.

I wasn't very nice when we met on the plane, and yet you

tried to be kind. You started a conversation with me, and were kind enough to find me and check on me after. Yes, a bit stalkerish, but also persistent and sweet. Although, I have to be honest, I didn't want to appreciate it.

Then, like some kismet way of the world, we were thrown together at the premiere, and again, you were nothing but sweet. Our abbreviated sushi dinner was one of the best I've ever had in a long time. But once again, I threw your niceties away in the trash because at the end of the day . . . I'm a bitch.

So, I'm very, very sorry. More than you will ever know, Layton. I have no excuses, nor are there any worthy.

I guess you were right. I'm not so happy with what I'm doing right now, but this was my plan, so I'm locked in.

That's about it.

Forever sorry,

Charli

P.S. I miss your videos and pictures of your dog.

I pressed SEND before I could regret it or second-guess it any more than I already had, and curled up in my perfectly lavender bed and fell asleep to the sound of Lucy humming.

Fifteen

Layton

Harriette lay in the corner, a paw covering her eye. Bingo! She didn't like it when I jacked myself. I know, I know, she's a freak of a dog.

Hey, I'm her master, and I assumed it was because she only liked to think of her and me.

Long story short, I'd been beating it pretty regularly all week.

I'd tried to drown my imperfections and insecurities in a cute, short-ish ginger after Charli hit the road—not the waitress, but a quirky, short, sci-fi-loving one more suited to me.

She laughed at my jokes and made googly eyes at me all night in the back of Bastion's; enough so, I felt bold enough to take her home. She lived in the neighborhood too, and led me up to her condo where I proceeded to be unable to perform.

Like, not at all. There was no movement whatsoever. My dick was set on an unattainable sexy blonde, and no pixie redhead was going to replace her.

I chalked it up to whiskey dick and hit the road faster than I thought possible. Carrie insisted on typing her number in my phone, and my fucking dick demanded I delete it.

This was a true story. I was legitimately addicted to a woman I couldn't have . . . not to mention she didn't want me.

Then I'd fucking heard from Charli on Tuesday, and while it was all business and nothing spectacular, my lower appendage was back to doing the thinking and making demands. Now I had a twice-a-day yank, Charli front and center in my mind, lithe and seductive but into me. Way into me. In my fantasy, she'd moan my name, scratch her fingers down my back, and tug on my hair.

Shit. And just like that, I blew my wad everywhere.

That was pretty much status quo. All because of a girl who couldn't even let me know she was home safely until four days later.

After wiping up, I let Harriette out and went down to my studio to get lost in my latest contract. I waited for my slow-ass dog to lollygag over before shutting the door to the soundproof space. If not, she'd scratch on the other side of the door and I wouldn't hear shit.

Slapping my headphones on my ears, I cued up the latest footage on my screen, rolled my mouse over several music selections, and double-clicked on the new song by some pop icon. The director wanted the song somewhere in the film, anywhere I saw fit, but definitely somewhere. It was probably his niece or some shit like that.

My computer was slow to load so I kicked my bare feet up on my steel desk and checked my e-mail on my phone, not expecting much for a Friday evening. Most people were out doing the happy-hour thing; I was sitting at my desk in a post-masturbatory funk like a complete loser.

Or maybe not? Because sitting right there in my in-box was an e-mail from Charli, using words like *kismet* and *sorry*, and just like that, I was on top of the world.

Sixteen

Charli

I wasted the weekend away at home, mostly in bed working on a collection of short stories I'd written a long time ago. I didn't exercise or go out for the salad bar. The hours ticked away with mug after mug of hot tea and the *tap-tap-tap* of the keys on my laptop.

By the time Monday came, I'd resolved myself to the fact that Layton took my apology for what it was worth and moved on.

From what? I didn't know.

I ran, showered, and took the subway to work. There was a newfound pep in my step from working on my stories, and I was early enough to grab a latte from the corner coffee shop. The streets of New York looked like a movie on fast forward—people rushing in and out, cabs honking, heels and loafers pounding the pavement.

Pushing through the revolving door of our building at Twenty-Seventh and Fifth, I noticed a pretty big crowd by the elevators.

"Hey, Sully, what's going on?" I stopped by the security desk, setting my latte on the counter while looking for my ID badge.

"Celebrity in the building."

"Oh?" I snapped my ID card on the front of my jacket.

"Yep, blond, skinny . . . aren't they all? She's got a movie out right now." He snapped his fingers, the corners of his eyes crinkling while he was deep in thought. "Seven sins of something or other. That's it!"

"Of course," I mumbled and all the pep evaporated from my step.

I sipped my latte on the elevator and made my way to my office, avoiding the cubicles of the entertainment department. They were all aflutter, and I wasn't in the mood to break my current mood.

I shut my door and after settling in at my desk, I pulled Lucy out of my bag. While I was scanning my e-mails, my phone rang.

Larissa. Of course.

"Hello," I said into the phone, knowing full well who it was.

"Charli, how are you?"

"All good down here. Getting ready to request some photography for September already."

"I'm going to pop down, one sec."

That's the thing with Larissa, she flitted around here, inserting her touch on everything. Her fun-filled, live-every-moment-to-its-fullest philosophy breathed life into *BubblePOP*, and she loved what she did.

I didn't always.

"Hey." Larissa peeked in and smiled broadly, looking like she just stole the last K-cup from the kitchen. "Katie is here today!" She actually fist-pumped the air. "You went to the *Seven Sins* premiere, and we need someone to sit down and ask her some questions and write it up. Can you? Sounds like you're working ahead anyway."

"Um, sure. I don't really do Hollywood interviews, though."

"It will be good for you. Show your breadth. Showcase all your pizzazz. You can handle it. Let's say, thirty minutes in the conference room?"

"I'll be there."

What was I going to say to my boss? *I don't have any pizzazz . . . because I'm not sure I like this job?*

I didn't think so.

Or *I don't feel like it because I had a connection with this guy, and I don't know how to handle that in relationship to my career and my past. I'm such a loser.*

Nope. I was going to down my coffee, interview Katie with a confident smile, and go home and curl up alone in my bed.

Seventeen

Layton

I cocked an earphone to the side and answered my phone when the caller ID read UNKNOWN. In la-la land, that wasn't very unusual.

"Griffin here."

"Hey, is this Layton Griffin?"

"Yep." I leaned back in my chair, knocking my headphones around my neck.

I was actually dressed for work today—it was Monday, after all—and propped my Chucks up on the metal table to the side of my desk.

"Great! My name's Ricky and I'm the music editor at *BubblePOP*..."

At the mention of *BubblePOP*, my mind traveled about a hundred miles an hour, quickly rendering images of the one person I knew who worked there.

"I'm sorry, you were saying? My phone broke up," I lied.

"Ricky from *BubblePOP* here. I know this is a bit out of left field, but the star of *Seven Sins of Serial Dating* was here this morning—"

"Katie?"

"Yeah—"

"Not sure what I can do for you, buddy," I interrupted again. Was this a prank? Did they know about my insane obsession with Charli?

"Well, it's a long story, but bottom line is this. The head lady here had Charleston interview Katie because she was at the premiere and all that lucky bullshit . . . pardon my French, but I really wanted to go."

When Ricky sighed loudly into the phone, I wondered if he was gay. What kind of guy wants to go to a romantic comedy?

"Anyway, Katie actually said this was her most favorite sound track of any film she's ever done, and well, I jumped at the opportunity to talk to her more about it. Yeah, I snuck down into the interview, but don't say anything. So, Katie turned to me and gave me those baby blues, all focused on me, and mentioned the Ed Sheeran song being her favorite. She said the music guy, who was so funny and nice . . ."

Nice? Yep, that's me. Nice. Not hot, or cool, or amazing. Nice.

"She gave me some awesome quotes, and now I get to run my own story on the music page, and yay!"

The sound of his clapping came through the phone.

"Sounds cool. What can I do for you?"

I couldn't believe Katie knew the name of my company and was able to tell this douche nozzle where to find me.

"So, Charleston interrupts the whole Katie-giving-me-ga-ga-eyes thing and pipes up that she knows you, and she thought it would be awesome for us to chat. Maybe I could ask you some questions?"

Charli gave him my number?

"Really?" I sat up in my chair, suddenly interested in what he was saying.

"Yeah, for real."

"Sure, dude. When do you want to do it? I assume you want to collect your thoughts."

"Um, yeah . . . that'd be great. Maybe FaceTime or something?"

"Whatever you want, buddy," I assured him.

"Cool. Charli said you'd be nice."

Of course she did.

Nice.

Ricky and I set something up for later in the week, and I hung up as despondent as I was when the conversation began. There was a moment in the middle when I thought I'd beat it again, and then I learned I was *nice*.

What did nice boys do? They took their dog for a walk, and this one walked and walked and got lost for hours.

I spent the better part of the week catching up for the hours I lost on Monday.

Eighteen

Charli

I shrugged off my cardigan as soon as I hit my office; it was an unusually warm May day and the building had yet to turn on the AC. Seated at my desk, I rolled my neck and blew out a long sigh. I'd been up late writing. Actually, I was quite the writing maniac lately, my creativity coming in long bursts, usually at one o'clock in the morning. This week alone, I'd finished the line edits on all six of my short stories.

A knock sounded on my slightly ajar door.

"Hey, Charleston."

"Hey, Ricky, what's up?" I leaned back in my chair and eyed my openly gay coworker who recently became my BFF because, as he said, he thought I had the "hook-ups."

"I'm meeting in a bit with Layton over FaceTime and wanted to see if you had any last-minute pointers."

"Nope." I shook my head. "He's seriously a really nice guy. Probably too nice."

Ricky eyed me curiously, raising a brow as he leaned on the door frame. "You know, toast is *nice*."

"What?" I laughed for the first time in a week. My mood was good and Ricky was kind of hysterical, and I was blissfully happy for a fleeting moment.

"Seriously, Charli, you're such a Brianna. You get all googly when you talk about Layton, and then you go and say, 'he's so nice' in some weird drawn-out breath like you're trying to convince yourself."

I had to roll my eyes when he flipped his hands up with exaggerated air quotes as he imitated me to perfection.

"Ricky, I don't even know what a *Brianna* is!"

"A babe. It's a babe, babe. If I were into female babes, I'd be all over you . . . babe."

"Ricky, not one more babe. We're at work." I waved a hand, shooing him away. "Go do your interview and shut my door."

He blew several air kisses my way and left me to my own devices.

God, he's the female equivalent of Janie.

I scrolled through my in-box. I had e-mails from Mom, Garrett (my mom gave him my e-mail address), the photographer wanting to set something up, but nothing from Layton since last week.

I slammed Lucy closed and stood up on my stilettos, threw on my cardigan, and made my way down the hall on the pretense of using the ladies' room.

Again, who was I kidding? I popped over to the media room, making my way past the celebrity-stalking writers, and like a bee to honey, I went straight to the music people.

Ricky's office door was closed so I paced in front of it, practically wearing a path in the carpet. One pass, two, three, four passes, five, six, and on the seventh pass, I knocked.

"Who is it?" came from behind the door.

I creaked it open an inch. "Hey, Ricky, it's me. How was your interview?"

As if I was that dense. He knew that I knew the interview was just getting started. For heaven's sake, it was only seven o'clock in the morning on the West

Coast.

"Ooh, lookee who's here." Ricky swiveled in his chair, winking at me before swinging back around. "Charleston, please do come in."

Directing his next words to his computer screen, he said, "Looks like we have a visitor. Layton and I were just chatting 'bout how he picked the music for *Seven Sins*, and believe it or not, he said the last choice came to him when he was seated next to you on a plane."

I slipped inside the office and peeked at Ricky's oversized monitor. Onscreen was Layton, wearing a Taylor Swift tee (*really?*) as he leaned against a graphite-colored desk. Behind him was a huge mess of sound equipment, stacks of discs, and wiring.

Layton frowned. "Well, that's not exactly what I meant to say. I don't want my words to get mixed up."

"Yep, you said . . ." Ricky sifted through his notes and flipped to the second page, where he began to read. "I finalized the song selection for *Seven Sins* on a flight from Chicago to New York . . . not to be included, that's where I met Charleston. The last song was killing me. It was for a hot, sultry, aggressive LA club scene in which Katie goes berserk on her man-to-be and another ex of his. I went with a newer on-the-scene rapper, Sumptuous, and took a risk with his first single, 'Bitches Cut Up.'"

Ouch. I dropped my gaze toward the floor, counting fibers in the burlap rug. *And I said he's too nice?*

Layton cleared his throat. "But let it stand for the record that I didn't mean Charli specifically."

"Oh, good," Ricky said as he made a note. "Thanks for clearing that up."

Ricky then returned his full attention to the monitor but I continued to stare at the carpet, bitterly regretting coming down here and wishing I was back in my office returning my mom's e-mail.

"Hey, Charli," echoed in the office.

"Char," Ricky whispered, snapping me out of my self-induced fog.

Dragging my gaze reluctantly back to the monitor, I said, "Hey, Layton. I didn't mean to interrupt . . ."

Actually, I did.

Layton narrowed his eyes slightly and said, "Good to see you."

When he leaned closer to the screen as if to see me better, I wanted to plunge into the depths of his eyes. I indulged myself by stepping a little closer but forced my hand to remain still and not reach out to trace his face.

Was that a slight tan? It suited him.

"Yeah, same. Honestly, I thought Ricky might be finished and wanted to debrief."

"Did you switch to entertainment?" His eyes bored into mine, mesmerizing me.

"Um, no. I was just being a nice coworker."

Ricky piped up, breaking the moment. "We're going to see the movie this weekend. I know Char saw it, but I didn't yet. I wanted to chat with you first, felt it would give meaning to it."

"Cool," Layton said with a tight smile. "Charli said she liked it, but you know, you can't believe everything a girl says."

A burning flush of shame scorched my cheeks. Embarrassment simmered in my veins, and I dropped my gaze again as I said, "Well, I did like it."

I started walking backward, my feet barely able to move, let alone in reverse, as I stammered, "I . . . um, I guess I'll let you two get back to it." I prayed I didn't trip in my heels.

I was such an idiot. Honestly, I might be this twenty-eight-year-old hotshot at work, but in real life I was an absolute stooge. My eyes filled and I quickly turned toward the door before either of them saw the first tear drop onto my pale pink sweater.

Boy, I was a sight. Little Bo Peep crying because of the Big, Bad Wolf.

"Hey! Charli," Layton called out. "I'm sorry."

I ducked my chin and waved a hand behind me, dismissing him and his hurtful words as nothing.

"Stop, seriously," he insisted.

"Char!" Ricky hissed at me.

I turned back toward the monitor to see Layton was leaned so far forward he was practically sitting on his desk, his face filled with tension.

What was I doing, stringing along some dude in California? For what?

"I'm going to finish with Ricky," he said, "and by the way, thanks for passing my info along, and then I'm going to e-mail you. I actually have another meeting back out there with a smaller label who's trying to woo me to use their music. Maybe we'll finish our dinner?"

I opened my mouth and froze for a second. Since nothing was quite making it out, I snapped my mouth shut and gave Layton a curt nod before I turned and got the hell out of there.

Nineteen

Layton

I spent twenty more minutes chatting with Ricky but my head wasn't into it. In fact, I couldn't remember a fucking word I said to him; I could have told him we were using nursery rhymes in the next film for all I knew.

Christ. I slammed my hand down on the desk, startling Harriette, who lifted her head off the dog bed and stared at me like the asshole I was. I was so mad that Charli had described me as nice, I'd subconsciously set out to prove her wrong. Or some shit like that.

I was fucking sick of being the nice guy when the arrogant pricks got all the great girls. I didn't want to settle for the quirky girls anymore, the ones who read paranormal fiction and loved Luke Skywalker. I wanted someone different from me, not the female version of myself. My head and heart—and my dick—craved something more, something different.

Charli, to be exact.

I could have sworn I saw a tear drop from her beautiful blue-green eyes, a tiny droplet so uncharacteristic of her hard shell. The sight of it filled my heart with so much regret, it nearly split it in half.

"Fuck!" I brought my hand to the desk a second time and toppled a stack of discs, mesmerized a second by their spinning pattern on the hardwood floor.

Frustrated, I stood up and threw open my studio door. "Come on, Harri."

I shoved my feet into an old pair of running shoes and snatched Harriette's leash from the hook. We took another long walk through town and back again, stopping outside the coffee shop for water. Most people walked their dogs to exhaust them—I walked to exhaust myself.

And I couldn't believe it, but after one week of walking, it was taking longer and longer to exhaust my fat ass. I needed to e-mail Charli like I said I would, but I couldn't bring myself to hide behind my computer with kind words when I'd gone all asshole over FaceTime.

By the time I had my head on straight, I'd done two huge loops with Harriette and was drenched in sweat.

When we got back home, I dragged myself into the shower, dried off, threw on sweats, and poured myself a bowl of cereal. Only half of what I poured interested me, and I ended up spilling the rest down the disposal and snatching my laptop.

FROM: LaytonG@darksidemusictracks.com
TO: Charleston_Richards@BubblePOP.com
SUBJECT: Harriette is disappointed in me

Charli –

Even my dog is hiding in shame from me. My actions today were not me. Asshole is too nice.

Cue head bang into desk.

And to think Ricky said you called me nice.

I would never call you a bitch. Yeah, I chose that song after our flight, but it wasn't directed at you. I don't know what I was thinking. Life's a bitch, or some shit they print on a T-shirt.

Forgive me?

I really will be in NYC next week, staying in Columbus Circle. I have to go to dinner with the label on Tuesday, but was hoping you could join me for dinner on Wednesday. A makeup dinner? Even sushi? Anywhere you want.

Okay, I'm rambling . . .

—Lay

I attached a picture of Harriette hiding her snout behind her paws and hit Send.

It had to mean something—me being seated in 2D on my way to Chicago and then again as I headed to New York. I slid into the leather seat and asked for a bottle of water rather than a drink; it was a Tuesday and I had to go straight to a meeting and dinner.

"Thanks," I mumbled to the attendant and then squinted at her. I must have had something in my eye because I was pretty sure she winked at me.

At me?

"Have a good flight, and let me know whatever you need," she said, and winked again. Maybe she had something in her eye.

Scrap 2D being lucky. It was making me crazy.

And then it got worse when a curvy redhead in a Princess Leia tee and hip-hugging jeans squeezed in next to me.

"Hey," she said on a breath.

"Hi," I muttered.

Ignoring her, I grabbed my laptop and headphones, busying myself with listening to some of the music repped by SoulTime Records, the label I was meeting with later.

"Ooh, I like that song." She reached across the center armrest and pointed at my screen. Her arm was covered in bangles and a large Darth Vader tattoo. My type. Usually.

"Oh, yeah?" I asked, my eyebrow raised.

"Yeah. That song, 'Loving Like a Hero,' is the bomb."

"Say it ain't so?" I said, my voice condescending and gruff.

She crinkled her nose up at my rebuff. When did I become a dick?

"Yeah." This time her response was muted, and I decided to never take seat 2D again.

Nothing good ever came of it.

My meetings were a blur of wooing, fancy food and beverages, and music. These SoulTime dudes meant business; they had a full roster of clients and they wanted to get maximum exposure. They'd gotten my name from a guy on a few movies back—that one had made the chick from reality TV famous, and I'd put her song in the credits.

Finally, back in my hotel room on Wednesday afternoon after twenty-four hours of being pursued, I sat down at the small desk, kicked off my Chucks, and opened up my e-mail. I'd purposely avoided checking it while in meetings. Mostly out of fear that Charli would cancel.

I had a few messages from the studio about filming updates and when they would be sending some footage, and there was the one I was both fearing and wishing for.

FROM: Charleston_Richards@BubblePOP.com
TO: LaytonG@darksidemusictracks.com
SUBJECT: Re: Dinner

Hi, Layton –
    Hope you are having fun here. I have a staff meeting until

six, and then I'm free. How about Chowww? It's close to where
you said you were staying, and I can easily grab a cab up that
way. I probably can't get there until about seven. See you then.
—Charli

That was all she wrote, and I started to climb the walls trying to decipher
what that meant. Curious, I googled Chowww and found it was a sushi
restaurant. *Shit*. But I'd gone and suggested that.

It was hip. *Shit again.* All I had was T-shirts and jeans, and of course my
Chucks.

But she hadn't said no. That was a start. She'd agreed to a second dinner
with me.

Pacing my hotel room, I found myself absently reaching for Harriette's
leash. Where was the damn dog when I needed her? And when had walking
become a source of tension relief for me?

Where was the freaking minibar?

Oh, fuck it.

I grabbed my earbuds and phone from the desk, shoved them in my pocket,
and stomped toward the elevators. Outside the hotel, I stuck in my earbuds and
hit the pavement.

With a bundle of nervous energy in my gut like a high school girl on prom
night, I crossed to Central Park and merged with a group of runners, joggers,
power walkers, and narrowly avoiding a bicyclist.

People passed me on the left and the right, and I quickly was lost in the pack
of pedestrians sweating it out in the park, but I kept walking. I passed an iconic
rock, the reservoir, and the dormant ice skating rink. It was closer to summer
than spring and the park was in full bloom, kids and New Yorkers getting their
fitness on and roaming every nook and cranny of the park, dressed to impress
in their brightly colored workout gear.

I stuck out like a sore thumb in my Converse sneakers, loose jeans, tee, and
hoodie, but I kept going. Soon, I was in the Upper East and then Harlem. I went

until the bend in the road and headed back toward where I came from. As I passed the Upper West, Central Park South came into view. As dusk fell on the city, I could see the rooftop of my hotel peeking out above the trees.

Drenched in sweat, I looked at my phone. *Fuck*, I had forty-five minutes to get to Chowww. I ran across the street to my hotel and headed toward the elevators before changing course to catch the attention of the bellman.

"Excuse me, but how far is the big loop of the park? All the way around?"

"Six," he barked.

"Six what?"

"Miles," he said curtly, frowning at me like I was the weird one.

Hmmm. Six miles, and I'd successfully avoided the minibar.

As I stepped onto the elevator, I fist-bumped the air. Harriette was in trouble when I got back home.

Twenty

Charli

I finger-combed through my layers in the cab and ran my tongue over my teeth before popping a mint into my mouth. Of course, we ran late at work and now I was stressing about getting to Chowww on time. Well, I wasn't, but I was silently wishing the cabbie would step on it.

Eh, I muttered to myself and sat back. There was nothing I could do, and why was I rushing like this for Layton? The last time I saw him, he was an ass. Of course, I'd been a bitch the time before that, but who cared? He wasn't my type, not even close.

My phone dinged.

> *Janie: You up for drinks?*
> *Charli: Can't tonight, have a thing.*
> *Janie: A thing? Be that way.*
> *Charli: Seriously. No biggie. Tell you tomorrow.*

She wasn't going to let this go, but I couldn't bring myself to tell her yet. How would I explain my unnatural attraction to the big dude? The one I'd sent out an SOS to have her rescue me from.

My phone dinged again, and I almost ignored it.

Mom: Why are you ignoring my e-mails?

Yep, I should have ignored it. My mom only resorted to texting when she felt it was the only way to get me to answer. She was sort of right.

Charli: Because I am not going to date Garrett.
Mom: Don't kick a gift horse in the mouth.

Oh God, she was getting all cliché on me, and to make matters worse, was mixing them like metaphors. I thought groupies avoided clichés?

Charli: No, it's just no. Love you. I will call you over the weekend.

I tossed my phone in my tote, refusing to look at it anymore.

Closing my eyes, I drew in a long breath. This was it. One dinner with Layton, and then I'd let him down easy and move on with my life.

I repeated the mantra to myself all the way to the restaurant, then flipped the fare toward the driver and hopped out of the cab at quarter after seven. Pushing through the double doors, I left the humidity outside for a thumping bass and cool air-conditioning.

As I made my way into the bar area, guilt ghosted over me. Guilt over predetermining how this evening would go. Shame over how I texted my mom, and even more guilt over leaving Janie in the dark.

"Charli!"

I heard my name called over the crowd and looked up to find Layton sitting on a couch, nursing a cocktail. He looked relaxed in loose jeans and an AC/DC

T-shirt, his legs spread wide, his hair mussed and damp from a recent shower. He would have looked badass except for the broad smile on his face and the excitement brightening his eyes.

Yes, I was a bitch.

Oh, and I'd suggested sushi without thinking, and I already knew he didn't like it.

Determined to shrug off my attitude with my coat and apologize later, I made my way over to where he was sitting and dropped my jacket on the sofa.

"Hey!"

"Hey!"

We spoke at the same time and chuckled awkwardly as Layton gestured for me to sit.

As I sat next to him, I was surprised by the heat radiating from his body. His scent titillated my senses, so fresh and clean with notes of rain, and I felt dirty taking my fill.

"I ordered a drink so they would let me keep the seat," he said, his tone apologetic. "I didn't know what you would want."

"Oh, that's fine. Sorry I'm a few minutes late, but . . . no buts. Work ran late and then I had to get a cab."

Layton motioned for the cocktail waitress, and I asked for a glass of cabernet before turning my attention to the guy in front of me. I drank him in despite telling myself he wasn't my type. Although, there was something different about him . . . a little bit of a tan and something else, a glow maybe? Did men glow?

"So, how've you been?" He cocked his head and focused on me.

"Pretty good, busy. We're throwing ideas around for the holidays already."

"Really?"

"Yep. It will be ninety outside, and I'm looking at ideas for low-calorie hot cocoa and how many calories we burn while sledding. Takes all the fun out of the season."

"Damn." He laughed, a warm baritone more genuine and relaxed now.

"How many calories do you burn sledding?"

The server brought my wine, interrupting my time to answer.

"Cheers." I clinked my wineglass against Layton's tumbler. "Something like four hundred."

"Wow."

"More than sex."

Layton raised an eyebrow, and it caught on a small lock of hair that had fallen on his forehead. I resisted an urge to run my finger through his hair and push it back. Instead, I gulped my wine to hide my embarrassment and nodded.

"Hmm, interesting. I may have to move where there's snow. Although Harriette likes the beach."

I giggled as if we did this every Wednesday after work. And every Friday. And again on Sunday over brunch. Sitting here next to Layton, our thighs brushing, no pretenses. Just us.

The nice guy and the bitch.

Beauty (*him*) and the Beast (*me*).

I swept back my negative thoughts and released the smile that so desperately wanted to come out. "Tell me about the elusive Harriette."

He winked. "She's my girl, tried and true. I love that bitch."

I gave him a fake scowl.

"It's what they call a female dog—"

"I know," I said, grinning as I interrupted his explanation.

"She's really pretty awesome. A buddy of mine got one of her littermates for his fiancé a few years back, and I went over for a drink and knew I needed one. The next day, I drove out to meet the breeder and came home the proud owner of a golden retriever."

"I've never had a dog," I admitted.

"Really?" His eyebrows perked up in disbelief.

"My dad worked a lot, and then when he passed away, it was just my mom and me. Too much work, I guess."

"Sorry to hear that. Your dad, not the dog thing."

He reached out and his knuckles grazed my cheek in sympathy, starting a shiver that ran down my whole spine and shot back up again. I gave myself a mental shake, shocked that I was ready to get it on from a tender touch.

"I grew up in Arizona," he added, "on the outskirts of Phoenix. My parents bought in Scottsdale when it was still cheap. We always had three or four dogs at a time, mostly little ones, Yorkies and Peekapoos. My mom loved them . . . I guess they were her company while my dad worked. But those little guys were low maintenance compared to Harriette."

"I couldn't even imagine having a dog in my apartment."

"One afternoon with my girl and you'll be googling breeders."

The conversation was getting too personal, too intimate and emotional, talking about his parents and his mom and his beloved dog. So I went for a topic change.

"How was your meeting?"

"It was pretty good. Cool guys, from Pittsburgh originally, and they have a pretty intense pipeline of up-and-coming artists. I liked what I heard, and I'm going to take it back to the producers."

I followed his hand, watching it lift his lowball glass to his lips, fascinated that he didn't have fat-person hands. I didn't even mentally chide myself for thinking that; I just watched in wonder as his strong hand, so large and well groomed, wrapped around the glass.

Layton's voice drew me out of my crazy hand fascination. "If you want, I'll send you a sample later. They're good tunes."

Snapping my gaze back to his face, I smiled. "I'd like that. So, is this movie romantic?"

"Nah, it's an action flick. I can't spend my whole life on romance."

"Why? You don't believe in true love and love at first sight?" I tried to sound as if I were joking, but I was intrigued. Intrigued enough to delve back into his personal life.

He almost choked on his drink as a small cough barreled up his windpipe. "Um, I don't know. That's not what I meant. I just meant I don't want to specialize in one kind of flick. You know, keep my options open and all that."

"Oh." I swallowed the lump that had taken up residence in my throat, clearing out more guilt. Why would he be thinking about love with me? "In this action movie, it's all hard rock or rap? No soft tunes?"

"Mostly, which is why I don't do all action either. My tastes are eclectic when it comes to music. I like it all, and when I do all types of movies, I get to use it all."

I took a sip of my wine, allowing the small burn to move down to my lungs, hoping to breathe free again. After all, I didn't like being stuck in fitness that much, but I wasn't bold enough to branch out.

"I get it."

I turned my head to the side, pretending to take in the DJ, and the shorter layers of my hair fell over my cheek.

"You do?" Layton reached out to brush my hair back behind my ear, searching for my gaze as if he wanted to see into my soul, to capture what I was *really* saying.

"Well, yeah. You don't want to pigeonhole yourself, to borrow a trite expression. I get it, you know? I used to be a full-fledged writer but now I'm stuck in this editing rut. So I get it."

"But do you want to write more than edit?"

Warmth crept up my cheeks. How was this man pulling everything honest and real from me? *Maybe because he's so real . . .*

I lifted one shoulder in a shrug. "I guess I do, but it's not that easy. I landed this job fresh out of school and here I am moving up the company ladder, and it's *BubblePOP*, which is the big leagues when it comes to online content. What would it look like to go backward, to set up shop in my apartment? I'm not Carrie Bradshaw looking for my Mr. Big."

Wait, that didn't sound right. I stopped my rambling and gathered my thoughts, hoping he didn't take that the wrong way.

Layton waited patiently for me to continue, his focus never deviating as his hand rested lightly on my knee.

"What I mean to say is yes, I'd love to write all the time, but I have to make a living." Frowning, I added, "But I'm not so happy making a living at what I'm doing now, and I sort of feel like I sold out."

I said the last part in a low voice, praying it was drowned out by the heavy music vibrating the room. For some reason, I didn't want to admit defeat or shortcomings to this guy. He was so confident, successful, had his shit together. Maybe that was part of the attraction?

"What do you write? Like to write?" Layton asked. Apparently he wasn't going to let this go.

I finished off my cabernet and closed my eyes for a moment, enjoying the way my belly burned, trying to channel some of his confidence.

"Mostly short stories, emotional ones all woven together in a common theme."

It was the first time I'd shared this with another person other than Janie. She'd nearly fallen off the futon cackling when I admitted to my "hobby" years ago.

"Wow, sounds like you've done a lot more than just thought about this. I bet you have a whole book written on . . ." He snapped his fingers. "Lucy! That's it, Lucy."

He didn't return his hand to my knee, and its absence felt like a gaping hole in my gut. I needed another drink. If I hadn't started with wine, I would have ordered a Scotch, but mixing never worked for me.

"Sort of," I lied. I had the whole book written. On Lucy. Line edited and ready to go.

"Want to get a table and finish this conversation?"

I nodded, wanting to say *I'd love to get a table, but I don't want to finish this conversation,* but something was stopping me. I liked it all too much. Loved it. I wanted to hold on to it for as long as I could.

Layton settled the tab with the bar waitress and stood, placing his hand on my lower back as he guided me toward the hostess.

"Do you have room for two?" He waved two fingers in the air and either didn't notice or ignored the brunette's sneer. He wasn't New York chic and wasn't even trying to be, a fact she clearly didn't appreciate.

"We don't have a table for two open," she said with a disdainful sniff. "Sushi bar only."

"Sushi bar's great," I chimed in, narrowing my eyes at the rude waif. "My favorite, actually."

"Fine. This way." She grabbed some menus and led us through the labyrinth of a restaurant.

"Wait, one sec," Layton called as we passed the signature Buddha. He winked at me and pulled me close for a selfie. "Say cheese," he whispered in my ear. "And take a long time so we really annoy the hostess."

I guess he did notice her attitude.

Seated at the sushi bar, we ordered another drink and a few rolls based on my recommendations. Layton begged and borrowed for an order of chicken spring rolls, which were not normally served at the bar. His quiet charm won out, and I watched him dip the crispy fried treats into duck sauce.

"About the sushi, I'm sorry. I suggested this place without thinking. I should have been more thoughtful. Italian or something would have been better, but this place, it's a New York must, and I didn't think about you."

He brought his palm over my hand and squeezed. "It's cool. I said sushi. No worries," he said, and it felt genuine and honest.

This man was too good to be true. Like a fairy-tale prince, he was rescuing me, not from a villain but from a life of boredom and mediocrity. What if that wasn't what I wanted? I'd worked so hard for so long for one thing, and one thing only. To get ahead.

So did I want to jump on his horse and ride away?

He enjoyed his food, savored it in a way no one I hung out with did. It was refreshing. I stared at his tongue dart out and lick his lower lip clean, and I had to mentally restrain myself from leaning forward and doing the job for him.

"Here, take one bite. It's not going to kill you."

Layton knocked me out of my trance, holding a small bite of spring roll in front of me. My tongue leaped at the chance to share the closest proximity with his fingers; it took every ounce of restraint in my body to keep it from running its tip along his thumb.

Only eat the spring roll.

I closed my mouth over the morsel and I might have moaned at the salty, fried goodness bathing my tongue in calories—a poor substitute for Layton's finger.

I should have told Janie what I was doing tonight; she would have talked some sense into me. Maybe I should have listened to my neurotic mother and met Garrett for a drink?

Because here I was having dinner with a man I met on an airplane, a happy-go-lucky, chummy type, warm and affectionate with eyes you could drown in. A guy who liked to make me laugh and shared witty banter; he ate fried food and had probably never taken a spin class in his life.

None of my attraction to him made sense. It was all a jumbled mess in my brain.

"Good, right?" Layton swiped his thumb across my chin, apparently removing a stray crumb.

"Really good."

"You're not going to run five extra miles tomorrow, are you?"

What's with this guy? Does he spy on me?

"Truthfully, I'll probably be tempted. I'm a fitness editor, Layton. Practice what you preach and all that."

"I guess I don't exactly fit the mold of who you normally share dinner with?"

He asked the question quietly, his eyes not meeting mine for the first time since I'd arrived. Instead, he concentrated on the mahogany bar in front of us, running his index finger along the edge—instead of on my knee.

"Layton . . ."

"I know. It was overly optimistic of me to presume I had a chance."

This time he stared at me, his wavering confidence nothing like the Layton

I'd seen thus far. I was beginning to think he wasn't human with his super-confidence, and this glimpse of his vulnerability only made me want him more.

He lifted his gaze to mine and gave me a small smile. "I just felt like taking a leap, trying for something I really, really wanted. Not something . . . someone. And that person is you, but . . ."

I chugged a healthy gulp of cabernet and when I put down my glass, I released it and bravely forced my hand to move over the dark wood and settle on top of his. We'd been having all these light touches through dinner—our legs brushing against each other, his hand roaming my knee. This shouldn't have felt electric, but it did.

My smaller palm barely covered his large hand, and the connection when we touched was explosive. Sparks flew between us, spurring me to lean in and kiss his cheek. I kissed the heck out of that cheek, my lips lingering on his scruff.

Oh yeah, did I forget to mention the scruff?

A thin smattering of stubble covered his chin and cheeks—dark and speckled, scratchy and silky, delicious and sinister. It had been calling to me all night.

And I'd just made the first move.

A fireworks display worthy of the Fourth of July above the Hudson erupted from just a kiss on the cheek.

"I'm glad you tried. You leaped," was all I said, running my thumb over the top of his hand.

An ember burned in my belly, shooting warmth down to my core and back up to my chest. What would his lips taste like? I wanted desperately to know but wasn't bold enough to make that move. Was I?

Would he?

His thumb wrapped over mine and held my hand steady. "Yeah? I mean, I want it to be true and I've been hoping all night. Each time you let me touch you, my confidence grew the tiniest bit, and . . . geez, listen to me running off at the mouth like a girl on Instagram."

"I'm in a weird place, Lay, but this feels more right than anything else right now."

"It's not because I'm a conveniently nice guy, is it?"

He swallowed, and I watched the lump of fear pass his Adam's apple.

I shook my head. It wasn't—I refused to believe that's what this was. I'd never wanted to settle. Now wasn't the time.

Grinning, he leaned forward and murmured in my ear, "Then this calls for cake."

"Cake? Really?"

"Really."

"Well, if we're going to go all out and I'm going to have run a bunch of miles in the morning to pay for it, how about one of those soft-serves in a cone? Have you seen them, the trucks all over Central Park? The best ice cream in America, and cheap."

It was my favorite treat, especially on a hot day after a long, long, long run. The type where you set out to do ten miles but ended up doing twelve because it was just so freaking nice out. Never after a date, though.

"Sold. Let me grab the check and we're out of here."

Layton captured the attention of the server, paid, and stood again, guiding me out of my chair and out of the restaurant with his hand on my back.

Pushing through the door into the warm New York night, skyscrapers looming over us as we walked toward Central Park South.

"So, this is the real deal?" he asked. "This ice cream?"

Layton's laugh echoed down the street, and I wanted to snatch it away from anyone else who might have heard it. I felt strangely territorial, wanting to keep his goodness all to myself.

"It's pretty damn good. Come on." I tugged his T-shirt, pulling him toward the corner. The hum of the food truck vibrated against traffic, horses clip-clopped and evening runners sped by us, and it was one hundred percent bliss.

"Two cones, swirl, please," I said to the guy behind the counter, pulling my wallet out of my tote.

"Hey." Layton swatted my hand. "I'm not that kind of guy. The going-Dutch kind."

I tossed a twenty on the counter. "Well, I'm that kind of girl. Besides, what kind of Big Apple host would I be if I didn't buy you a treat from a street vendor?"

I took a long lick of my cone, moaning as the creamy coolness made its way down my throat before I even put my change away.

"I'm not waiting any longer if it's that good." Layton brought his tongue out to meet the ice cream, mesmerizing me again.

"Want to walk?" he asked while I shoved my change away and grabbed a light sweater from my bag.

Chills were forming from ingesting the cold ice cream, coupled with the searing heat between us. I put one sleeve on while licking my cone and then switched. It wasn't even close to being glamorous or seductive, but it was never about that with Layton.

With him, I could be the socially awkward girl who was way too ahead of herself, but was afraid to admit it.

We ended up walking up Central Park South toward Columbus Circle, eating until there was nothing left and swapping stories. Somehow we got stuck on the topic of peanut allergies, I think because of the nut vendors on the street and different people we knew with the ailment. We agreed that while it was serious, the whole not-serving-peanuts-on-an-airplane deal was overboard.

Then again, we weren't parents, so what the hell did we know? Honestly, it was such meaningless banter yet heavily weighted with meaning, simply because we were doing it. Chatting like a longtime couple with plans for a future and kids with allergies.

At Columbus Circle, I stopped in front of the Time Warner Center. "Pretty sure this is you."

"It is."

We stood there quietly, no more laughing over peanuts and long-gone ice cream cones to busy our hands with. After an awkward moment, he broke the silence.

"We could have a drink. You could come up?"

As he watched me, waiting for an answer, I studied him back, nearly sighing at how his brown eyes looked like a warm honey amber against the twinkling skyline.

Oh. My. God. I was a cheesy girl falling for a guy, the star of my own romantic comedy.

"I'd like to," I answered, grinning from ear to ear. "Want to play me some of the music you heard today?"

His face lit up like the Empire State Building. "You'd want to do that?"

"I would."

He linked his hand with mine and practically dragged me into the hotel lobby and toward the elevators.

Twenty-One

Charli

We rode to the seventeenth floor and made a right off the elevator. I should have felt awkward going to Layton's hotel room, but I didn't.

He stopped outside a corner suite and pulled a key card from his back pocket, then slipped it inside the door and popped the lock open. "Welcome to my humble digs." He held the door for me, turning the privacy lock after we were both inside.

"Pretty sweet suite," I joked.

For one or two beats, I wanted to run, to go home and snuggle with Lucy, but then Layton looked at me. Not with his usual smile, but an entirely different expression. It looked like hunger or a need to be close—a look I'd really never experienced before.

"Let's have a drink." He took my hand and led me to a small sofa in the sitting area. "Let me see what the minibar has in stock. Sit," he said, commanding and calming my nerves, but doing little to cool my hormones. "There's cab or a pinot noir, or would you like something stronger?"

"Cab is good."

I watched his hands, the ones I was becoming more and more fascinated by, open the travel-sized wine bottle and pour it into a glass and then open a small bottle of Lagavulin and toss it into a lowball glass.

"I always think those minibottles are so cute, like they belong to Barbie or something."

"I always think they could be a bit bigger," Layton said, carrying the drinks to the couch. He sat and handed me my wine. "Cheers! Again, I'm damn happy it didn't end like last time."

"About that . . ."

"Don't." He winked. "Don't ruin this with an explanation."

"So, back to la-la land tomorrow?"

He nodded.

"Who's with the infamous Harriette?"

I wondered if he had someone he was seeing in LA. He was the kind of guy someone snatched up and didn't share, right? A good, dependable guy. Kind and considerate. Just the right amount of command and take-charge.

"My neighbor. She loves Harriette."

I felt the corner of my mouth turn up and willed it to change direction. No such luck. Happiness ghosted through my veins.

"She likes the company since her son went to college. She and her husband are good to Harri. They walk her, give her lots of love. I'm lucky."

"Oh?"

"I mean I'm luckier to be here now."

Another *oh?* slipped from my mouth. What was I fishing for with this guy?

"Yeah." Layton leaned over and took my wineglass and set it on the table, placing his tumbler next to it. He ran his hand down my cheek, a small callus on the side of his thumb grazing my skin.

"I want to kiss you. Is that okay?"

Molten pools of chocolate stared at me. All I could think about was when I was ten years old and my parents took me on a trip back east. We stopped overnight in Hershey, and I remember wanting to dive into the vats of chocolate . . . just like I wanted to dive into Layton right now, despite him being all wrong for me. A lot like chocolate, I guess.

My overachieving brain was running circles inside my head. Pros and cons floated around in there, jumbling with my hormones, but the hormones were winning. Thank God.

"You should," I whispered.

And he did.

Layton leaned in, and the scent of clean rain filled my senses as he touched his lips to mine. They weren't too soft or chapped, but were just right, tasting mine with a confident firmness. At first, his kiss was simple, chaste even, not demanding anything from me as he watched me through half-closed eyes. I drank in his gaze for one last second before closing my eyes and allowing the sensations to overcome me.

He inched closer, and I basked in his warmth as his knee bumped mine and his hand came down to rest on my leg. He brought his other hand up to sift through my hair, eventually allowing it to settle on the back of my neck, keeping me close. And he never let go of my lips.

A small nip at my lower lip encouraged me to open my mouth and allow him to deepen the kiss. When I did, his tongue swept through my mouth, looking for mine and tasting like chocolate ice cream.

God, sinful chocolate. It was all I could think about, a big sundae of all my naughty vices—the guy and the chocolate candy and the ice cream.

We stayed like that for a while, kissing and exploring as we sat on the sofa. Both of us needing to breathe, we broke free for a minute and stared at each other as our chests rose and fell in sync.

What was Layton doing to me? I met the guy on a plane in a down time in my life, and despite the fact that I wasn't nice to him, he pursued me through e-mail. I had to be the dumbest girl in America despite all my academic and business success.

As we gazed at each other, saying nothing, his hand roamed my waist at the bottom of my shirt, his thumb tracing the fine line of skin at my waistline. His finger was smooth against my skin, never snagging or scratching.

It was heaven, I decided, but not for me.

"I have to go. This is a lot to take in, okay?"

Layton's eyes widened. "I'm sorry if I pushed too fast. Stay, Charli," he said while scooting to the far side of the couch. "I'll keep my hands and lips over here."

"It's not you, it's me."

Mortified, I grabbed my forehead and took a deep breath. "I did not just use the most cliché line ever, did I?" I mumbled, refusing to look up for fear shame or regret would be plastered on Layton's face.

"You did, but it's cool. I get it. This is unexpected."

I looked at Layton sitting there, his AC/DC tee stretched across his chest and riding up a smidge on his hip, his dark hair a mess, his jeans unfashionably loose, and those Chucks.

Could this be me? Here with this guy? Then I saw his dimple and the stubble and the way sincere worry transformed his face, and I thought . . . yes, it could, but I didn't know if I wanted it.

"I have to go," I repeated. "I just need to collect my thoughts."

"Okay," Layton said, but he didn't move.

"I'm going to catch a cab downstairs."

Please e-mail me.

Please don't hate me.

Keeping those thoughts to myself, I stood and grabbed my tote, noting my half-full glass of wine on the table. *Is my glass half-full or half-empty?* I was starting to believe I was a half-empty kind of gal.

"Do you want me to walk you down?"

I shook my head. "Thank you, but no." I headed toward the door.

"Why don't I stay an extra night?" he suggested. "We could do drinks here, on the rooftop of the hotel. I hear it's pretty outrageous at night. We can just relax, have a couple of drinks, and end this on the right note. Not like now."

"Okay."

I might have agreed but I knew I wouldn't show up. My inner bitch was winning out, and I hated her. I deserved a lifetime of being alone. I had to get out of there.

"Seven again?" he asked.

God, he was still trying. He was so nice. "Sure."

I gave Layton a quick peck on the cheek and ran right the hell out of there—my lips furious at me for rushing them away from his perfectly stubbled cheek.

Part 2

Twenty-Two

Layton

Eight Months Later

I half sat, half leaned at the bar waiting for her. It was an overpriced, cliché hole-in-the-wall in Manhattan she'd suggested. *Best burgers in New York*, she'd written in her e-mail. She'd assumed I'd want something big and heavy to eat, overselling the place to me and avoiding the fat fucking elephant in the room.

Which was me, so I didn't take the burger suggestion as a slight. I deserved that one. Especially after the sushi debacle.

But I wasn't one bit hungry for burgers—not tonight. To be honest, I was famished for her. I was so fucking starving for this woman, I'd gone without an apology, showed up like a good little puppy without even as much as an apologetic whisper. No *sorry* or a single freaking misgiving about what had happened the last time we saw each other. Zip.

Now I sat in the bar area like one of those big whales at Sea World, waiting in line for a dead fish. It was dingy and dimly lit, but the Yelpers loved this joint.

Of course I'd googled it, making sure I was hip enough to show my face in the establishment.

Impatient, I swirled the Scotch in my tumbler, the ice clinking against the glass. Out of habit, I pulled my shirt down at the waist, making sure it covered my waistband. It was a habit I still couldn't quite shake. I'd worn a waffle-knit shirt and khakis, the new trendy kind, elastic at the ankle and a drawstring at the waist—all the bells and whistles.

I wasn't sure why I felt like I had to forgo my usual look. The only other times we'd met up, I'd been wearing a music tee and jeans. Except for the premiere, but tonight was different from the other times . . . I hoped. That assumption was probably false and premature on my part.

As I took a sip of my drink, the liquid burned the back of my throat and warmed me all the way going down, heightening my arousal and calming my nerves at the same time.

Tiny bells chimed above the door, signaling it was opening—a touch that was out of place for New York City, but I assumed it was part of the charm of this joint.

She stepped over the threshold, shaking the snow off her now longer hair before swiping her gloved hand down the front of her coat. I saw a hint of red peeking out from underneath her black coat, reminding me it was just past Valentine's Day, making me wish I'd come earlier in the month. She could have been *mine*.

She still hadn't seen me, so I indulged in a second or ten, allowing my gaze to roam her small frame all the way down to the fur-lined ankle boots . . . with a heel . . . on her feet.

Unable to get up or move toward her for fear she'd reject me all over again, I turned back toward the bar and caught the score of a basketball game on TV while tossing back the remainder of my Scotch. I felt her presence singe the back of my neck before she laid eyes on me.

Willing myself not to turn and seek her out, I ran a hand through my hair and mentally chastised myself.

You pussy. Just look at the woman.

My hair was styled the same, so she should recognize me from the back. At least, that's the sorry excuse I gave myself.

I didn't look, just forced myself to remain focused on the game. It was close, 82–75. Who was I rooting for?

Who the fuck was I kidding? I didn't even watch basketball. The last game I remember watching was the NBA playoffs the night she didn't show all those months ago . . .

When the clock had struck eight, I'd pretty much known Charli wasn't coming. I'd extended my stay in New York, moved my return flight to the next day, and bought an actual button-down shirt on Fifth Avenue. But the whole day, a hint of her reticence when she'd agreed to tonight gnawed at me.

She wasn't going to come—I knew it. My heart knew it. I felt it in my fucking bones. But I still bought the shirt like a chump, cleaned up my stubble, and shoved my feet in my Chucks like a man in love.

I'd found a quiet corner of the rooftop bar, where the corners of the glass met each other in a seamless line so as not to obstruct the view. I asked for a Scotch and then changed my mind to a beer, and seconds later changed it back again . . . to a Black Label and soda. My finger traced the flawless seam while my eyes roamed the New York skyline, but I saw nothing other than my reflection. Chubby cheeks, messy hair, and a shirt that was too tight.

My legs ached from yet another long walk in the park. I'd scrubbed the BO off in the shower, but my heart still beat too fast. Whether it was from the anxiety of waiting or my lack of fitness, I didn't freaking know.

What I did know was Charli wasn't showing.

And she didn't. She didn't even send an e-mail or a text to explain her absence until two months later. There hadn't been an accident or a situation at work. She just couldn't bring herself to come.

On the television, someone in white and orange ran down the court and slam-dunked the ball, and a commotion broke out in the bar. I squinted and looked closer. It was the Knicks playing. Made sense. I continued to ignore the tingling at my back, the heat seeping up my neck, singeing my hairline. She was there, looking for me, and I was being a dick.

I set my tumbler on the bar, left my jacket on the back of my chair, and stood, turning to face her. She was standing at the back of the bar, her coat now thrown over her arm, and her hair longer and spread down her red sweater. Her cheeks were pink from the cold and her lips a glossy red. She was pristine and perfect, everything I wasn't.

"Charli," I called out, annoyed at the frog in my throat.

She looked up and caught my eye, and her brow furrowed. "Layton?" She stepped closer, her boots eating up the floor.

"It's me."

We stood facing each other, the bar stool a deserted island behind me. I wanted to slip back onto it, disappear from her inspection.

"Are you okay?" Her eyes took me in with concern, not hunger or need.

I wanted to look at the floor, but I was stronger than that. I kept my gaze on her and remained firm and collected.

"I'm fine. Actually, more than fine."

"You look so different. I mean, you look great, but I thought that maybe you were . . . sick." She stumbled over her words, pausing to collect herself like an amateur, not a professional wordsmith.

"Healthy as a horse." In fact, I felt like a stallion in certain places. Namely my dick.

"Wow," she whispered as she averted her gaze, unable to meet my eyes.

"Want to sit?"

"Sure. Sounds good." This time she was the one with a frog in her throat.

Perhaps a couple of frogs, judging by the scratchiness in her voice.

I pulled out the stool and she slid onto it, and I took the empty one next to it.

"What would you like? Wine?"

"Honestly, I may need something stronger."

She pushed her hair behind her ear, revealing a large hoop earring. That was new. In fact, as I took a closer look, I realized she definitely looked more casual, carefree even. Chunky bracelets lined her arm, rather than the understated chic jewelry she normally wore, and the bright lip gloss was definitely new.

"Charli, I'm okay. I don't know what is upsetting you. I lost weight. A lot of it, actually, but I'm good. Seriously. It's a good thing." Words ran out of my mouth like surfers into the ocean back home.

"You look good. Really good. I don't know, I guess I was expecting funny and humorous Layton. The version I hoped would forgive me for what I did, but now I'm sitting here shocked and I've totally forgotten what I wanted to say."

The bartender interrupted our moment. "What can I get you? Another Scotch?"

"Cosmo, please," Charli said.

"Beer this time. Amstel Light?"

"You need a glass?" he asked, and I shook my head.

"I'm still the same Layton," I told Charli, consoling her rather than welcoming the apology I so badly wanted from her but didn't get.

My hand wavered until it settled on top of hers. Her fingernails were painted a delicate pink, gentle like her heart. She might have bruised me, but it was only an attempt to protect her own weakness. I'd figured that out while soul-searching during one of my many jogs. She was only putting a wall up around her ego, not strong and self-assured like you'd think, but stunted and fragile.

The bartender set down her drink and she took a healthy gulp. "Um, you're definitely not the same Layton."

I took a pull of my beer and set it down so I could study her. "I was kind of hoping that'd be a good thing."

This wasn't going the way I had anticipated. We were having a stilted conversation, avoiding the new reality. I was now good-looking Layton, and she was expecting desperate Layton. Did she think I wouldn't forgive her? That I had moved on?

Well, guess what? I was still just as desperate to forgive her . . . taste her . . . have her.

She smiled and leaned forward to whisper, "You're really sort of hot."

As she leaned close, her scent filled my nostrils. It hinted at vanilla, reminding me of cupcakes and flavored coffee creamer, and nearly drove me crazy.

I squeezed my hand at my side, desperately needing to get a hold of myself.

"Is that bad?" I asked.

She shook her head.

"So, what's the big deal?" I took another sip of my beer.

"I liked you the way you were before." She gulped down the martini and met my eyes. "I was just afraid to admit it. It's not that you were ugly or horrible. The opposite of that. You were so nice and warm, like a teddy bear. But we were so different, and I felt like I held too many cards or something. The big job, the looks or whatever, and I didn't want you to feel like . . . less of a man." A fiery blush flared over her skin at her admission. "I don't mean that in a bad way or a condescending way—"

She broke off, seeming flustered. "God, I don't even know what I mean. But if anything, you made me feel inadequate. Because I was."

What? Was she crazy? Charli would have the upper hand no matter what. She was a desirable, smart, and sexy woman. After all, it had been eight months since our last contact, and she dived right in for the kill. No small talk, zip.

Wasn't that what I craved?

"You're too analytical, Charli. Life isn't like an editing job where all the t's have to be crossed or the i's dotted. It's like a mix tape, a compilation of all the best hits, some slow and others fast. Some songs aren't your favorite, but mixed with the others they make a great album. It's all in the placement."

Charli sighed and gave me an earnest look. "I wanted you to know that I wanted you for *you*. But I couldn't express it in a way that wouldn't come out awful or rude. And now you've gone and changed yourself, and I can't ever make peace with that. I can't let you know how I felt and how I agonized over not showing up. Not without it sounding like a lie."

She shoved her hair behind her ear, and I noticed something else new.

Right below her earlobe, on the smooth slope of her neck, sat a small tattoo. A symbol. I couldn't concentrate on that thought because for the first time in months, I allowed myself to breathe. One word—*agonized*—and I was breathing easy.

She agonized over me, and while that should make me uneasy or ashamed, it didn't. Some twisted sense of pride washed over me at the mere fact she'd been thinking of me.

"Hearing that makes me feel better, seriously. So much better that you considered me." I couldn't let her hang all the guilt on her own shoulders, though. "But this whole thing wasn't entirely about you. I needed to feel good about myself and so I changed my appearance, but not who I am. I'm still happy Layton. Happier and healthier, that's true, but the same."

Charli focused on her glass. "Well, I was in a bad place, not liking my job, obsessing over appearances. Now I'm in a happier space too," she said slowly, and then raised her eyes to mine. "A lot of it has to do with you."

"Oh yeah?"

"I went home after running out of the hotel and spent two days in bed. No running or spinning. No drinking with friends. Just working from bed and thinking. I'd turned into a shell of a person, a drone on a path of self-destruction. I hated who I was, and I decided to make changes."

She took the last sip of her drink and I swallowed the dregs of my beer.

"Want to get a table," I asked, "so you don't have to rush in telling me everything?"

"Um, do you still eat burgers?" Her cheeks were as red as her cashmere sweater.

"You betcha. I'm dying for one." I pinched her cheek. "I'm not a waif."

We stood and asked for a table. The hostess looked me up and down, hungry in a way I wished Charli was. Being dismissed was not one of the things I missed about being fat.

We were shown to a corner table in front of a large picture window. The table had a graceful lily in a bud vase, and Sinatra played softly in the background. A runner brought sparkling water and slices of lemons and limes. I poured us each a glass and sipped mine, allowing the bubbles to clear my throat. It was clogged with a mixture of frustration and hope.

"So, tell me more," I said. "I haven't seen you since last summer. I want to hear it all. Your days in bed and how you're not a drone, because you look fucking fabulous. Not that you looked bad before, but whatever you're doing now, it looks great on you." I let it all hang out there.

Charli took a deep breath and met my eyes. "Well, I didn't like running from you, but it was too heavy, too much for me to handle. I left home at sixteen and a half for school. I always knew I didn't want to trade everything in like my mom, but I also wanted passion, heat. Crap, I didn't know what I wanted. Back in your hotel room, I realized I wanted you, but I was so far away from what I wanted for me. My career wasn't what I wanted, and well, you weren't the type of person I ever imagined myself being with."

Her hair had grown out. Layers still framed her face, but it was longer, more feminine. For the briefest of moments, she looked fragile.

"Sounds like you did a lot of soul-searching," I said, trying to keep my tone light. "I don't know if I've ever done that much."

She laughed and her giggle filled the restaurant, overshadowing Sinatra, which was close to impossible.

"Yeah, well, about that. I had some savings, plus some money I had from my dad's insurance when he died, and I quit my job. It probably sounds pretty spoiled, but I think he would've wanted me happy. At least, I picture him wanting that. And so I spent the summer and fall sitting in coffee shops, writing . . . and thinking."

"Sounds pretty awesome—"

I got cut off by the server who rattled off a few specials, touting the burger of the night—Wagyu beef with fried onions and wasabi mayo on an onion brioche.

"I'll give you a few minutes, but drinks? A refresher?"

"Another cosmo?" I asked Charli, wanting this asshole to go away. When she nodded, I said, "Cosmo and an Amstel Light."

I wasn't driving and I was being bad with a burger, so why not drink a bit?

"That's why I didn't e-mail or anything for a few months. I had to get my life together. And then by the time I did, the words escaped me in what to say. I figured you'd moved on."

Her blue-green eyes shone brightly in the soft lighting. I wanted to skinny-dip in them, and I'd never considered baring myself to someone in that way. Body and soul.

"Well, I guess that explains your lukewarm apology."

"I didn't want to be too assuming . . . I never imagined you'd wait for me. I wasn't that important or whatever. When you reached out, I said yes right away."

I'd e-mailed her on a whim. A funny thing had happened on the set—there was a dog and he was doing a trick but ended up barfing—and I couldn't stop laughing. The actor was so disgusted. Without thinking, I attached a video clip to an e-mail and asked to see her, asked for a chance to make her laugh in person.

She'd agreed, and I booked a flight. It was a bit risky, but I had to know if she liked the new version of me.

Apparently, she liked the old one.

I spent several beats staring at her, drinking her in. She was better than beer or Black Label. Way better than the most expensive bottle of champagne.

"Okay, here you go." The server set our drinks on the table and asked, "You ready?"

"Well, the burger of the night feels like the way to go, but the onions? I guess they only work if we both eat them?"

It was a veiled question, a wimp's way of asking what I wanted to know. Did she like the new me in *that* way?

"I'll have that," Charli said.

"Two specials," I said to the server, and then looked back at her. "And fries?"

She nodded. "Of course."

"And fries to share," I told him, mentally adding, *And now, scat.*

Charli swallowed, and I braced my hand on the table. More than anything, I wanted to run my hand over her skin, allow my fingers to trace her collarbone. I wanted to pull her close . . . to kiss her.

Nothing with this woman was meant to be rushed. She was like a fine wine that only improved with age and time. Time she hadn't been given growing up, but I'd waited close to a year.

I could wait some more.

Twenty-Three

Charli

He stared at me, his eyes melting me, turning me into a gooey mess.

I showed up expecting witty Layton, the guy who liked to make me laugh.

Instead, I found hot and sexy Layton, who still made me laugh. Of course, he'd been handsome before; I could see beauty beneath the girth. But this? This was unexpected.

I had no idea how to react, the appropriate thing to say or do. Did I say *holy shit you're hot now that you dropped fifty?*

Or *I thought I liked you last time I saw you, but now . . . whew!*

At first, fear ripped through me. I thought he was sick or something because he seemed content with who he'd been before. Why would he go and change?

"So, tell me about you," I said, changing the subject. "We've been talking about me forever." I'd spread too much out there about myself, and here I was trying to let go, love life, be free, and he shows up all tight and insanely dapper.

"To be honest," he said as he swirled an ice cube in his water glass and leaned forward, "this all sort of came about because of you." He took a long sip from it before he added, "Don't freak out. It wasn't to get you or anything like that."

I raised an eyebrow and felt it touch my bangs. "Get me?"

"I mean, it wasn't to win you over. I didn't feel like I had to change my looks for that. When I first started pursuing you through e-mails . . . yeah, kind of stalking you . . . I kept screwing up. So I spent a lot of time walking, more than I'd moved in a long time. By the time I got to New York that last time, I was already down a few pounds and feeling better."

"Funny, I was a fitness editor and obsessed with everything fitness, and now I've sort of let it go and you're all gung-ho. Life's strange, isn't it?"

He dropped his elbows on the table and leaned in even closer. "Let me be very clear, Charli. No way you've let anything go. Pardon my language, but you look fucking fabulous. You have since the day you stepped on the plane." He reached out to tweak a piece of my hair. "And this longer hair? It suits you."

When did Layton become so irresistibly bossy? And when did I start to love it?

Like five seconds ago.

Chills ran sprints up and down my spine, and butterflies were doing plyometrics in my belly. Between my legs, tingles and spasms took charge.

I had to say something, had to acknowledge him. "Thank you. Honestly, it's more of not having time to deal with it. Going to an office, I had to keep up with my hair. Now I tie it up and hit Starbucks."

"Don't change a thing. You're perfect, Charleston."

My full name rolled off his tongue and straight to my core. It had never sounded so delicious. I rubbed my palms along my jeans and smoothed the front of my red sweater, trying to wipe away the tension flitting through me.

"So, you're walking and feeling good, and then what?"

"I got into it. I was on that action flick, and started checking out the workouts the actors were doing when I stopped by the set. One day I asked to join in, and Ryan Richards, you know him?"

"Um, yes. Every female with a pulse knows him."

"Well, he took me under his wing. Literally. I was his charge. He set me up with his chef and had me doing all these workouts."

"Wow."

"Are you wow-ing over Ryan or the workouts? Because I never know. The last date I had, she wanted to know if I could introduce her to Ryan."

All I heard was *the last date I had*. I felt my lips press flat and my brows draw in.

"You don't have to feel bad if that's what you wanted to know too. I can introduce you." He took a long slug of his water, refusing to make eye contact. I'd hurt his feelings, but not intentionally.

"No, no, that's not what I meant."

"Here you go." Our waiter was back, arranging our burgers on the table along with some ridiculous french fry platter with a million dipping sauces. I wished he'd fall through the floor.

Stupid waiter.

When he left, our food sat there untouched as tension swirled between us. So I gathered my courage and spilled the truth.

"I don't want to meet Ryan. I guess I didn't like hearing you were on a date, but I don't own you."

"Charli, I've wanted to date you since you sat down in seat 2C. Are you not catching on to that? It's still me, Layton, and I'm still desperately trying to woo you. There may have been dates but there's been zero wooing. Only hoping for you."

Something unfamiliar pricked at my eyes, emotions I'd never felt. I couldn't unravel the ball of feelings in my chest.

"Come on," he said, keeping his tone light. "Eat your burger and tell me what's going on with you. What the hell are you writing? And then we can get some ice cream from one of the street vendors."

He picked up his burger and took a bite, and I couldn't help but watch him chew, the way his jaw flexed. I noticed he wore the stubble again.

Oh, that stubble. I'm a goner.

Wiping my mouth after a decent bite of burger and a fry, I said, "I submitted my collection of short stories. I got like thirty no's and then just like that, two deals came my way. The book is coming out at the beginning of the summer. I just approved the cover."

"That deserves a wow! And now what?"

I turned my focus to the table. I didn't want to admit this out loud.

Layton's index finger lifted my chin and raised my gaze to meet his. He raised an eyebrow in question.

"I'm writing a love story. A beauty and the beast kind of thing . . ."

"Well, I'm flattered. You're writing our tale."

Except I'm the beast.

I didn't say anything. I ate a fry and changed the subject, asking about the movie he was working on.

Dinner passed with more small talk and laughter. As we stood up from the table, our hands didn't know where to go. I wanted his to find the small of my back; mine wanted to find his other hand and weave our fingers together. Neither happened, but he did hold my coat up and I slipped inside, buttoning up tight.

When we walked through the door, cold air blasted us.

"I'm pretty sure it's not an ice cream night," I remarked, feeling a little sad at the prospect.

I didn't want the night to end, and I didn't know when he was leaving the city. I knew he'd met with the small music label again, and I assumed he would be out of here tomorrow.

My time was up, and the irony of the situation struck me. We were like a strange flip-flop of the classic fairy tale, but I was the prince and he was Cinderella at the ball. Soon he'd transform back to who he was and slip off into the night, leaving me alone.

I didn't care if he became the old Layton. I only didn't want him to slip away.

He gave me a somber look. "I guess I owe you one?"

We stood outside on the sidewalk, flurries swirling in the air, taxis whooshing by, and a herd of elephants surrounding us. Passion and hesitation flowed between us in equal parts.

"Want to come back to my place? I make a mean hot cocoa," I blurted before I could change my mind.

"Lead the way," he said, his relief palpable, and I waved for an available cab.

We hopped in and I rattled off my address. As the cab sped us to my place, we sat side by side in the backseat, thigh to thigh like we had on the plane, both of us staring forward, refusing to look at each other because of those damn elephants.

Then his hand reached for mine. I'd put my gloves on, but I still felt the heat of his marvelous hand through the cashmere.

And I wanted that heat everywhere.

Twenty-Four

Layton

I was going with Charli back to her place, something I'd never dreamed possible. I tried to calm down, needing to control my heart rate; it was beating faster than during any workout I'd ever attempted.

As I slid into the cab first so she didn't have to slide across, I scolded myself. The only thing on the menu was hot cocoa, and I wasn't such a big fan of the stuff anyway.

In the dim light of the cab, I studied Charli's features. She looked unsure of herself, unsettled. Not with the choice to invite me over, I didn't think, but more with what my intentions were. She'd met me at the restaurant to tell me she liked me the way I was, and I was a totally different person when she arrived.

Hoping to soothe her, I reached for her hand, engulfing her gloved fingers in mine, and relief passed over her features. Mission accomplished.

In front of her building, I handed the driver a wad of cash and we ran toward the door. She fell into my shoulder as she punched in the security code to the building, and sparks flew in the air, floating with the flurries. I wrapped my arm around her as she led the way to her unit.

I wasn't sure why I was so giddy. I lived in California and she lived in New York. This couldn't go anywhere, even if she wanted me. The old me or the new one, it really didn't matter. We were just too damn far apart.

"Come in." Charli broke the silence as we stepped inside her loft, hanging her coat on a rack and reaching for mine. She stepped out of her heeled boots, leaving her feet in pink socks with red hearts, and her height cut by two or three inches.

"Want me to take off my boots?"

"That'd be great," she said over her shoulder, walking toward a small kitchen area and flicking on the lights.

The place was basically one open living area decorated in various shades of purple and cream. I assumed a bedroom and a bathroom must be tucked somewhere in the back. I glanced around, impressed; even a California boy like me knew that for New York standards, the place was posh.

When she pulled a can from the cabinet and asked if I liked milk or water with my hot chocolate, I said, "Why don't you make some for yourself? I'm actually not a huge fan."

"Oh." Quickly regrouping, she stuck her head in the fridge. "I have beer, water, wine, but no soda."

"I'm good."

Not meeting my eyes, she busied herself, leaving a mug of water in the microwave to heat as she pulled out a tea bag. I came up behind her and caged her against the counter, my hands splayed on the counter and my front to her back. I wasn't forcing it; she could move if she wanted, but she didn't.

I ran my nose down her cheek and breathed deeply, trying to control the fire raging inside me on this cold winter's night. We stilled for a long moment, not speaking, me soaking her in through all my senses.

"I like you, Charli," I said softly, and I immediately wanted to take back my words. Rejection ran through my veins. It had happened before, and I didn't think my blood was still tainted with it. But it was.

She stared at the counter, her dark blond hair cascading forward around her face, the nape of her neck in plain view. Unable to resist, I kissed it, ran my lips over her skin like I had every right. Some type of urgency prompted me to touch her. Feel her. Inhale her. Do it all before she pushed back.

"I want you in the worst way," I admitted. "Ever since you sat next to me on the plane, my thoughts are a traffic jam of you. I think of you at the premiere in red. The way your fingers held chopsticks over sushi. My imagination runs wild, visualizing you reading my e-mails at work, in bed, or on your phone. Your smile. My head is like the 405 at rush hour when it comes to you. You're in my head, and I never wanted to be stuck in traffic so badly."

"Layton," she whispered.

I lifted one hand from the counter and swiped her hair away from her profile. Just a breath away from her cheek, I noted the tiny crinkle next to her eye, the swipe of glitter on her cheek, and the small mole next to her ear.

"Please don't push me away," I begged.

"Layton." Another whisper. "How can you want me? With how it ended last time? And how will you ever know that I really wanted you before you were a sexy god?" The side of her mouth turned up in a small smile.

"Turn around."

"No."

"You think I'm a sexy god?"

"I do."

"Turn around."

She twisted in my arms, but her gaze dropped to my chest. A tiny crease appeared between her brows when she said softly, "How will you ever believe that I'd come to realize I liked the old you?"

"It doesn't matter, Charli. I'm still me, and you're here and I want you so bad."

"Kiss me." Her words were soft, breathy, and her eyelashes fluttered the slightest bit over her half-lidded eyes.

I tipped her chin, needing to see her. When our eyes met, I was certain they were mirror images of hunger and want.

My heart pounding, I bent down and put my lips to hers. I kept the kiss soft, closed-mouth, a feather of a touch.

She stood on tiptoes and pushed for more, so I took it even deeper. She let out a breath and my tongue slid inside her mouth, tasting her. Wasabi and cranberry from the cosmo commingled with her strawberry gloss, and I was ravenous for more. She was soft, silky perfection, not like me. I was rough around the edges, but I pushed my fears of snagging on her to the back of my mind. I wasn't going to let my jagged imperfections get in the way.

The microwave beeped, her tea long forgotten, disturbing our moment. I wanted to take a baseball bat to it. Charli simply raised her hand, hit a button, and brought the hand back to wander my cheek.

I leaned forward and whispered in her ear. "God, what you do to me. Do you get it? I've been chasing you across the whole country just for that moment."

Her knuckles grazed my chin, my stubble prickling her smooth skin. "I'm sorry we waited so long."

"I'm not. Good things are worth the wait. The best is worth waiting even longer."

"You're the only one who ever got to me, made me believe I could have it all."

"You can," I assured her.

But could I? Where was this going?

I refused to let my overactive mind ruin this moment so I bent back down to taste her, my hand weaving through her long hair and around her neck. I kissed along her cheek and jawline, licking and sucking my way to her ear. I ran my nose over her skin, inhaling her scent, stopping right at the tat.

"What's this?" I nibbled on her ear, unable to make my lips or teeth stop.

"Some people call it the maloik, or the evil eye," she said, closing her eyes as she tilted her head back. "It supposedly wards off evil curses and provides protection and clarity. I needed it for me. To remind me not to curse myself."

My lips grazed the eye and murmured, "Christ, you're perfect."

My erection pressed against her stomach, and when I leaned into her, she climbed my leg so it hit her where it mattered. I grabbed her ass and lifted her, thrilled when she wrapped her legs around my waist and moaned.

My hand found its way inside the back of her jeans, exploring the globes of her ass. Firm, smooth, more perfection. Then she pressed harder into me, and for a second, I feared blacking out.

She pulled back an inch and murmured, "Let's go to my room."

"Which way?"

"Back there."

I carried her, her legs locked around me, our mouths fused.

She hit the light switch as I crossed the threshold, revealing a bed that was a sea of lilac and pillows. I laid her down and used my arm to swipe the pillows on the floor, and then I simply stared at her for a beat. Charli, her chest rising and falling, her hair splayed all around her in a golden wash over the lavender, her lip gloss smudged on her lips.

I stretched out next to her, still in the habit of not lying on top, even though I hadn't fucked someone in months. There were only two women since I'd met Charli—one-night stands, blah and boring. My vision turned red for a moment as my thoughts ran to Charli with someone over the last few months.

"You okay?" she asked, pushing the hair off my forehead with her delicate fingers.

I nodded. I knew better than to start this talk right now. She didn't think I was going to forgive her; she wasn't going to wait for me. And I didn't think she'd ever walk back my way with how fast she ran away.

I slipped my hand under her sweater and explored the expanse of her smooth, flat stomach. Inching up toward her breasts, my finger traced her bra as my mouth found hers again. I wanted to get closer, to feel it all.

"Can I take this off?"

This time she nodded and I tugged her sweater over her head, then slid my hand over her hot pink bra. I pulled the right cup down and made my way toward her nipple with my tongue. I licked and laved, sucked and nibbled. She moaned and arched. It was a wet dream come to life.

Charli turned a little more on her side and ran her hands under my Henley and up my back, skin to skin. I stopped kissing her to rest my forehead on hers, and took a deep breath. I knew what was coming and braced myself.

She pulled my shirt off, keeping her eyes on me the entire time. I stared back, hoping she wouldn't look at my body. I wasn't sure why; it wasn't so bad anymore. A little extra skin around my love handles. A scar on my pec from when I fell playing soccer when I was little. Someone's cleat caught my shirt, digging right through it into my flesh, and I needed fifteen stitches.

I was so caught up in my memories, Charli caught me by surprise when she ran her tongue over my flat nipple, her finger tracing that scar.

I took her hand in mine and held it tight between our bodies as I shifted closer. We were skin to skin, except for the bra. I unhooked it and ran my free hand down her back into her pants and pulled her close. We ground on each other like a couple of teens afraid to get caught with their pants down.

"I still think there are too many clothes involved," I murmured against her lips. I felt her nod and moved our connected hands down.

She went for my belt and I went for her button fly. We made quick work of them and shimmied out of our pants. I used my foot to divest her of the skinny jeans caught around her ankles and then she returned the favor, not a hot or sexy move but it did the trick. She yanked my pants down and flung them in the air. It felt familiar, almost like something we did at the end of every day, and for some reason that thought warmed me.

"Fuck, you're stunning."

I ran a hand over her ass. Her thong was hot pink, like her bra, and rested perfectly on her ass crack. I pushed her on her back and straddled her, taking my time once again with her mouth, but my tongue itched to taste her.

Was that too presumptuous? My dick lurched in my boxer briefs, encouraging me to hurry and sample her. No way was I doing that. If there ever was a moment to take my time, it was now.

I inched lower, my body sliding down hers until my tongue came into contact with her hard nipples. I circled each one and made my way down her stomach. The tip of my tongue trailed her vanilla-scented skin, leaving goose bumps in its path. When I breathed across her stomach and traced the lacy edge of her underwear with my tongue, her back arched off the bed.

In my life, I'd never been so happy to get the green light. I tugged her pink panties down and feasted my eyes on what was in front of me. A dusting of a landing strip shimmering with wetness—I assumed for me.

I had to think of something quickly—geometry, calculus—because my load was about to blow. It had been years since I'd done that in my boxers and right now, just the picture of Charli spread for me, glistening and groomed, was doing me in.

I traced her lips with my finger, and unable to stop myself, slid one inside her, floating off to paradise with her moan. I ducked my head and followed the same path with my tongue. Working in sync with my finger, the two reveled in each arch of her body in response.

Without warning, she came on a long breath, releasing my nickname into the air. "Lay."

"I got you."

She continued to vibrate against my mouth and then tugged on my hair. "I want you."

I wanted to ask her to say it again, but I couldn't force myself to admit I needed the affirmation.

My heart pounding like a fucking drum, I lifted off her small frame and found my jeans, taking a condom from the back pocket and ripping the packet open. I shoved down my boxers and gloved myself, feeling her watch me from under her long lashes, the biggest fucking aphrodisiac ever. Then I moved back on top of her, carefully bracing my weight on one elbow and guiding myself to her with the other hand. I slid in slowly, relishing each second. Every inch brought a wave of new sensation, another palpitation in my heart.

When I was fully in, I stopped and closed my eyes. It was too much. The beauty of her beneath me, the ache in my balls, the longing to go hard, the desire to stay balls-deep inside Charli was too fucking much. All it took was one roll of her hips and I started moving, and when I opened my eyes to see the gorgeous woman below, I found her eyes fixed on me.

Me.

With every thrust, she kept running her hands all over me, up my chest and down my back, finally gripping my ass as she threw her head back on a long moan and I couldn't wait any longer. I spilled myself, filling the condom, and when my breathing finally slowed, reached down to make sure the sucker stayed on as I pulled out. I removed it, tied it, and tossed in a small garbage can next to her bed, and gathered Charli in my arms.

Kissing her, smoothing her hair, I asked, "Was that okay?"

She buried her head in my chest. "Why did we wait?"

"Stop," I said.

"Now I'll always wonder if it would have been this good then—"

"Shhh," I said. "It's perfect now."

Holding her close was the closest I'd ever been to heaven. As she lay there nestled against me, I pulled her tighter, unable to believe how lucky I was.

But I'd never even dreamed she'd want the old me.

Twenty-Five

Charli

I lay sated on the bed, my hair a rat's nest, my inner thighs sticky and aching, and I couldn't move if you paid me.

What if this and *what if that* ran through my head. What would it have been like before? To make love, to fuck Layton? Would I have been on top?

"Hey, come here," he called from my bathroom, forcing me to discontinue the litany of what-ifs roaming the open plain of my mind.

I shimmied out of the bed and wrapped myself in a chenille throw. Pushing the door semi-open, I said, "Yeah?"

"Come here," he said, this time softly.

I walked into the bathroom to find the tub almost filled, steam rising off the water as Layton poured a small bottle of shower gel under the spout.

When he looked up at me, his eyes were burning with hunger again. "I thought you might like to relax in here."

He'd pulled his khakis back on but hadn't buttoned them, letting them ride low on his waist, revealing a small trail of hair that led to where his now familiar penis resided.

"You good?" he asked.

A warm blush crept up my chest at being caught staring.

I nodded. "I'm good. That actually looks so incredible . . . amazing actually."

"Great. Get in," he said and held out his hand.

I wasn't sure if he meant he was coming in after me or what, but I took his hand. The blanket fell to the floor, and he held me steady as I stepped in one foot at a time and slid down into the warm bubbles.

"Want a candle?"

When I nodded, he grabbed a book of matches from the tray holding my favorite candle and lit it, releasing a hint of persimmon into the air.

"You relax. Do you have any wine I can open? Or do you want some water?"

I shook my head. "No, but there's a bottle of champagne chilling in the fridge."

He went out, leaving the door slightly ajar, and I missed him already.

Tomorrow he'd be back in California, miles and miles away.

Closing my eyes, I leaned my head back into the neck pillow and willed myself to relax. That was tomorrow. But tonight wasn't over yet . . .

After we had the champagne, I lay cuddled on the couch with Layton, bundled in my fluffy robe. It was after one o'clock in the morning, and unease pummeled through my veins like the subway underneath the city.

What should I do? Should I ask him to get dressed? Kiss him good-bye? As my mind spun, I yawned.

Layton reached across my small couch to push my hair away from my eye. "Tired?"

I nodded. "A little."

His hand went back to rest on my knee and then slid down to my feet, which were curled on his lap. "Want me to leave? I don't want you to feel uncomfortable."

A rush of air pushed out from my lungs, a pent-up breath I hadn't realized I was holding. With it gone, the tension seeped from my body, leaving me feeling boneless.

"I hate to say this," he said, "but maybe I could push my trip a night and we could have those drinks at the top of my hotel. We never got to do that. The view is unrivaled . . . except maybe only by you."

"Want to stay?"

"Yeah." Layton brought his knuckles back to my cheek and caressed my skin. "I would."

He grabbed my hand, and we stood together and walked back to the bedroom. I straightened the comforter from our earlier activities and pulled it back. He pulled off his khakis and I watched from under heavy lids.

As if we'd done it a million times before, we crawled into bed and he pulled me onto his chest. His heart beat a constant rhythm much like his personality. Strong and steady. I curled in closer and closed my eyes.

His lips brushed the top of my head. "You didn't answer about me staying one more day."

"I'm afraid that tomorrow I'll wake up and this was all a dream. You're not real. Not here."

"I'm here and I want to stay longer. Does that work?"

I nodded, my hair grazing his chin.

"Good," he murmured.

It's the day after that I'm not sure how it will work.

We fell asleep wrapped in each other's arms.

I would have to worry about tomorrow after today.

Twenty-Six

Layton

I woke up with a start, not sure where I was. My dreams had taken me far away from home, landing me in the bedroom of my fantasies. *Although I never knew it was purple.*

Then I saw her—awake, propped up on an elbow and staring at me, a smile on her face and her hair tousled over her forehead.

"Morning," I grumbled.

"Morning."

"You good?" I asked, reaching out to swipe her bangs out of her eyes.

She nodded. "Want breakfast?"

"Maybe some coffee. Do you have to work today?" I asked her as she slipped out of bed, still snug in her robe. I wanted to tear it off and dive deep inside her.

"I should do a little, but not all day."

As I wondered if she'd want to hang out during the day or only at night, she said, "I could show you around parts of the city or we could go for a run?"

"A run sounds awesome."

I said that. A run. Me.

"Great, I'll make some coffee. Then we could run in Central Park since you need to go change."

It felt so normal, Charli suggesting a run and my accepting as if we did it all the time. But tomorrow we wouldn't be doing it.

Couldn't be.

That was tomorrow, I told myself.

We ran through the park and stopped for lunch before I went back to my hotel and Charli went to work. When she left, my soul felt barren. Seriously, as soon as she was gone from my side, I felt empty.

I was like Puss in Boots, tough, all macho and good-looking, but a softie at heart.

If the day went quickly, the evening felt as if someone had punched a button to fast-forward. We were having drinks at the bar on the top floor of my hotel, surrounded with floor-to-ceiling windows that showcased the skyline twinkling in the background.

There wasn't enough time for Charli's laughter or for me to appreciate the inquisitive look she wore when we discussed something important. At one point, she asked about which movies I'd worked on recently.

This time I didn't run my hand down the window seam like I had that night I'd waited for her here alone. Instead, I traced her kneecap, a small patch of bare skin that peeked out between her almost knee-length skirt and her knee-high boots. It was so soft, like a peach on a hot summer's day.

No, that was her pussy. And I fucking loved peaches.

Her knee was like silk sheets, fresh from the wash. I liked those a lot too.

Shaking my head, I mentally reminded myself I was a man. A horny one, but a man, and I should act like one.

Still, my finger stroked her slight kneecap and ran inside the top of her boot, tracing the top of her firm calf. I was as hard as a rock, my dick pushing against the zipper of my jeans, and I willed myself to get my mind off her pussy and concentrate on her question.

"After I finished on the action flick, I took a week off and got my head straight. That's when my fitness really took off. I was walking and walking; poor Harriette was exhausted. I fired my dog walker and walked some more. Then I picked up the gig with Ryan. Of course, it was a sexy comedy. It's coming out soon, by the way. He felt sorry for me, I think. When he was done with me, I was a new man. Now I'm working on that vampire movie."

She clapped her hands and bent over her thighs. "Oh my God, you're not?"

"I am."

As I sipped my Scotch, she brought her wineglass to her pink-glossed lips. I studied her, noticing the tiny trail of blush that decorated her cheek, and how her lashes met the pale pink shadow lining her eyes. She was so delicately beautiful, I had to close my eyes against her for a second. The woman took my breath away.

Her giggle brought me out of my stupor. "That is literally *the* movie. I actually read all the books. They're like free tortilla chips and salsa. Once you start, you can't stop."

"I've heard them compared to crack cocaine. Anyway, I'm learning all about the shimmering vamp and actually, the guys here are working on getting me a piece of music for a specific scene."

"Wait!"

She brought her small hand down on my jean-clad knee. A fire burst through the denim, heat soaking my entire body. That's what this woman did to me after one night.

"Are you going to this premiere?"

I laughed, the deep sound echoing around us. "I'm sure."

"Oh, I'm going," she said. "I can't miss that."

Grabbing her hand, I pulled the back of it to my lips and placed a kiss on her smooth skin. What I said was, "Of course," but what I meant was *thank fuck, you want to see me again.*

And that's pretty much how the rest of the evening went, up until we ended up tangled in my sheets in my room downstairs.

Softly illuminated by the moonlight streaming in through the gauzy window shades, Charli set her head on my chest and brought her leg over the sheet, laying it gently on top of mine.

"So, now what?" Of course, she was the one brave enough to ask.

"This was magical. I know it sounds foolish, but I mean it."

She nodded against my chest. "It was," she whispered.

"I'd like to see you again. I can come here; you can come to me. Would that be okay?"

"Are you going to be a whole different person next time I see you?"

I ran my hand through my hair and tucked my palm behind my head. "No. But honestly, do you think I'm a different person?"

She shook her head this time. "You're you."

"And I'm your guy."

Her hand lingered on my nipple, tracing circles. "My guy," she muttered and began moving her hand south. "Hey, I don't know your birthday. When is it? How old are you? I know you're older than me . . . ugh, I guess it's a little late to be asking."

"Turning the big three-five on September twenty-eighth," I said, her hair tickling my lips as I spoke.

"No way!" She snuggled deeper into my side. "Mine's the twenty-sixth. I'll be thirty—blah. Thirty, it's kind of crazy hearing it."

"Prettiest, sexiest almost-thirty-year-old I know," I said with a laugh but then sucked in a breath.

My body was at attention almost immediately from her touch. I wasn't sure it could happen again so soon, but apparently with Charli, my body knew no limits. Her hand wrapped around my girth, not fitting all the way but squeezing and pumping until I couldn't take it anymore.

I shoved her ambitious fingers away and crawled on top of her, then made my way down to her peach. Yep, I'd confirmed earlier it was as ripe and luscious as a peach, and I wanted to feast on it again.

Her back arched and she shoved her hips into my face before demurely pulling them away. I grabbed a hold of her hip bone and kept her still with my face planted right where I wanted it.

"Don't be shy."

She twisted in my grip, but I held steady until her whole body shuddered under my lips. As she lay there gasping, I climbed up her body, reaching for a condom and not wasting any time. Especially since she said, "Hurry, Lay."

I slid inside her and forced myself to slow down, taking my time pulling in and out of her, long and slow, appreciating the sighs coming from her.

Bending over, I whispered, "I'm your guy," in her ear before I picked up speed.

She came again, this time holding tightly to my back, her small breasts smashed into my chest, burning an imprint into me.

Twenty-Seven

Charli

Saying good-bye was hard. When I walked into the bar earlier in the week, I thought Layton and I would have a good time and share some quick laughs. That's it. I never expected him to spend the night—or to look the way he did.

God, I had just made up my mind that I liked him. He was witty, funny, and caring. And now he was freaking gorgeous.

It made me take pause and question who I was . . . even more than I'd already done. I'd certainly judged the hell out of him when I first saw him on the plane. Torn between my mom begging me to date Garrett and Janie's criteria for the type of guy I should date, I didn't want to like Layton.

But I did anyway, and had fought it by ditching him via an SOS call from Janie.

He continued to remain true to who he was, a nice guy, and I had finally come to terms with that. And then bam! Suddenly he was a hottie too.

My phone rang early on Sunday after Layton went back. He'd flown out

Friday afternoon, needing to get back because the movie was behind schedule and they were shooting today. It was a pivotal scene and he needed to be there. Otherwise, I was certain he would have stayed.

Or maybe it was wishful thinking on my part.

"Hello, J," I said, sipping my coffee. I'd been up, staring into space and dreaming of my time with Layton.

I'd turned into *that* girl.

"Come on, we're going spinning and then for brunch," Janie said. "You're going to fill me in whether you want to or not."

I stared at my bare feet, my pink-polished toes splayed on the hardwood.

"Janie . . . really?"

"Really. See you at the spin place in an hour. We're gonna sweat our butts off and then your mouth is gonna be running."

"Okay."

I hung up and tossed on a pair of leggings and a to-and-from-yoga top, threw my spinning shorts and shoes in a bag, and filled a water bottle. Janie had been hot on my trail since I mentioned Layton was coming.

Janie greeted me outside the spinning studio without even a hello. "You're the one who went MIA for forty-eight hours . . . don't give me that look."

"It's freezing out here," I said, ignoring her comment as I hoisted the door open. I went straight to the changing room and plopped down on the bench to remove my UGGS and put on my shorts.

"Charleston, I thought something happened to you. If I hadn't seen your picture on Instagram on Thursday of your run with him, I would've called the police." She shoved off her lululemon leggings, no shame in being commando, and tugged on mini biker shorts.

I actually heard a small note of panic in her voice as she sat down next to me, and felt horrible about not touching base with my best friend for days. I broke girl code.

"I'm sorry. I just got so swept away. And, well, Layton is hot now."

"Um, I can see that in the picture. Even with that blurry filter, I can make out all his hotness."

"But he's also so kind and funny, and really genuine. He's a good one."

She ran her hand down my hair, braiding and tying it, when I bent over to put my shoes on.

"I'm truly sorry I worried you. He blew into town like a hurricane and then stayed a day longer, but he had to leave and go back home. I sat staring at my laptop like a jilted woman yesterday."

She stood and tugged my hand, gathering me into her arms.

"You're crazy silly, Charli. You're a girl *in like* and I forgive you, but next time I'm going to call the cops. You had me so nervous, I could've spit, and I was pacing like my mom waiting for her brisket to be finished."

I laughed. "Come on, let's spin, and then we can chat over coffee."

"I have to go somewhere where they have almond milk," Janie said as we left the locker room, clicking in our spinning shoes.

"Oh God, what now?"

"Listen, not all of us are so lucky to work out and eat what we want and then find love."

I punched her arm.

"Okay, find *like*. But seriously, you're such a happier person now that you write and eat a bit more. Me, I've got to watch my Jewish thighs. Lord help me if I gain another ounce. So I cut out dairy."

"That's nuts, but okay. Only almond milk for you."

We spun, changed back into our clothes, and wrapped our sweaty bodies in our coats and walked down the street to a small coffee shop in the Village. We ordered and found ourselves a private table in the corner so I could tell Janie the whole story.

Well, most of it. I kept what Layton did with his mouth to myself.

I also kept my growing panic over how I didn't deserve him to myself.

Twenty-Eight

Layton

The week dragged on. The producers were adamant that we wrap filming, and they were bugging me day and night for tweaks. In between redoing the sound track, I ran miles, logged a few more miles with Harriette, and obsessed over Charli.

I wanted more than anything to be back there in her apartment, rolling in her lavender sheets with her in her pink panties and glossed lips. If I concentrated, I could still smell her on my shirt, but it wasn't enough. Still, I had a job, one I'd worked hard for, and she was doing her thing. It was what it was.

What would be enough?

I e-mailed her every morning and she usually responded right away because of the time difference. We'd only spoken twice, and planned to get together in two weeks. She was going to come here for Saint Patty's weekend, which scared the ever-loving shit out of me.

Did she expect to meet my friends? They were pretty much all I had since my parents were older and lived in a nursing facility.

Weird, I'd never even told her that. Would she care? Would she think I was callous? Maybe that's why I didn't say anything. Would she think my friends were dorks?

The questions tumbled in my head as my feet slapped against the pavement. I would need a new pair of running shoes by the time she showed up in March at the rate I was going.

I dropped down on the grass in front of my place and did one set of twenty push-ups and then another, alternating with sets of sit-ups. It was my own version of boot camp adopted from my workouts with Ryan.

Sweat dripped into my eyes and I swiped it away before going after my push-ups like a man in prison and they were my only purpose of the day.

Charli had mentioned that her friend Janie wanted to meet me. What would she think? I was pretty sure she was the one who was involved with that whole rescue-me gig at Zao's.

Christ, I was fucked.

I was back in high school all over again, plotting out some weekend party on the bleachers, and I hated it back then. What made me think I'd like it now?

Twenty-Nine

Layton

Two Weeks Later

Nerves were threatening to knock me over as I leaned against the wall in baggage claim. I was that nervous. Despite e-mailing, texting, chatting, and the occasional FaceTime session, anxiety wormed its way into every one of my body's cells as I waited for Charli to arrive. The last time, I was prepared for disappointment and/or saying good-bye. But it had ended way better than I could have dreamed.

Now she was coming to see me, and it could go one way or another. My gut said another.

"Hey!"

I startled, so deep in thought I didn't even see her approach.

"Hey." I wrapped my arms around her and squeezed her tight. Apparently my limbs had a mind of their own when it came to Charli.

We've been intimate, I reminded myself. *It's okay.*

She collapsed into my embrace, our body heat mingling through my jean jacket and her thick sweater, and seventy-five percent of my nerves dissipated. Maybe if I got her naked, the rest would go away?

No, that's not the point. She's not here for only sex.

"You good?" she asked me.

Shit, I'd been crazy caught up in my head.

"I'm good, just thinking about how awesome this is. You're here. For a moment, I was convinced I was dreaming."

She pinched my arm. "I'm here."

"You have bags?"

"Of course."

We walked over to the carousel and waited, a pregnant pause hanging between us.

"You know," she said, "I heard that for every two minutes of a conversation, there's seven seconds of silence."

I pulled her in again and kissed the top of her head. "I'm sorry. This just caught me by surprise, how happy I am to see you. I mean, I knew I'd be happy, but this is different. Overwhelming. And it's early."

"In a good way, I hope? Good overwhelming?"

"Extremely good."

"By the way, don't mention early. I'm on East Coast time, and I've already flown here from JFK. Do you know how early I had to be there?"

I kissed her cheek, tucked her hair behind her ear, and whispered, "I'm a lucky man for it."

She ran her palm over my cheek and smiled. No words were needed to convey she was happy to be here. The clammy sweat on my palms dried up.

"So, what's going on?" she asked. "What's our plan?"

And just like that, the last few lingering nerves flitted away. I didn't even need sex. Just the idea of us having plans.

"Well, it's Friday, so most of the guys try to cut out of whatever they're doing early. So happy hour later. But first, maybe a little tour? Lunch? Quiet time?"

She waggled her eyebrows at me. "You know, I also heard that men think about sex every seven seconds. We wrote a piece on it at *BubblePOP*."

"That's a nasty rumor. It's actually every nine seconds."

We both laughed so hard, we bent over clutching our stomachs. And just like that, we were back to being long-time friends and newfound lovers.

"Oh, there's my bag," Charli said, interrupting our giggles.

Settled in the car, I put on Calvin Harris and rolled down the windows. It was a gorgeous day—no smog, clear blue sky, crisp air. Charli looked like a movie star meets an angel or something like that in her big shades and her hair whipping around her face, sticking to her lip gloss.

I already wanted to beg her to stay. Not to leave. We would send someone to her apartment to pack her stuff and ship it out.

"How about breakfast food?" I asked her. "I'm sure you have to be hungry."

"Sounds good."

I shifted gears and willed my hand not to run along her thigh, but it did anyway. Her warmth burned through her leggings, and all of a sudden they were too thick. I wanted them off.

"You look great," I told her.

"I finally cut my hair. I had to compromise somewhere between the *I go to the office every day* look and the *I'm a homeless freelancer*."

"Pretty sure you could never be *that* look."

"I know. Actually, the weekend my mom came to visit, she dragged me to a salon."

"Ha! That's sort of funny."

"You weren't there. She has this thing now with me being a professional. It's so crazy because she was a groupie, wandering all over the country when she was in her early twenties. If she hadn't met my dad and fell in love, she'd have gone on being a hippie, I'm sure."

"Maybe she wants something different for you. Parents can be weird."

"Eh, I don't know. She's sort of making me nuts. All of a sudden, she's not supporting my wants."

"I can't say I have experience with it. Mine only wanted to see me grow up. Once I graduated college, they both went downhill so quickly."

Her fingers laced through mine. I had told her during one of our late-night phone calls about my parents. My dad, no memory. My mom, no mobility. Together, they were a whole, but only half a person on their own.

Charli had said, "I wish we were chatting in person so I could run my hand up and down your back rather than compete with the static on the line." She'd actually said that.

She was beautiful inside and out, and again the nerves were back. Not nerves about being with her, but fear of her leaving. I couldn't let her slip away. Not this time.

Our fingers were still twined together, but I had to downshift and turn into the diner. It was one of those classic LA institutions with jukeboxes on the tables and a black-and-white checkerboard floor.

"Oh, wow, I just realized how much I want a cup of coffee," she said when I came around to get her car door.

"It was a long flight. You left New York at five."

She grabbed her tote from the floor and shrugged out of her sweater coat, leaving it on the seat.

We walked into the diner, my arm around her, my heart in her hands.

"Two," I said as I flicked up two fingers to the hostess.

We were seated in a booth, and I let her slide in first. I sat across from her and our hands met over the table.

"This is sort of odd. It feels so comfortable, like we've done this before and it's part of our routine." She smiled as she spoke, her hair falling over her right eye.

I used my free hand to swipe it back and said, "I know. It's all the e-mailing and talking. I feel like I know you better than I know myself. By the way, how's the book?"

"It's coming. I still can't believe I sold the short stories, let alone signed a deal for three books."

I'd read her stories, against her protests. She'd sent them to me after I begged, and those suckers were good. Not at all sappy like you'd think. Real, poignant, and full of pressure or something. I didn't know the right word.

"What did they say your stories are full of?"

She laughed. "Angst."

"Right, I was just trying to remember the word. Char, your stories are great. Your book is going to be even better. You're a writer. Live it."

I wasn't sure why I felt poetic all of a sudden. She did that to me.

"I can't really compare to anything out here."

The waitress came over and took our order. Coffee, spinach-and-egg-white omelets, rye toast, fruit. Yep, I ordered that.

"Maybe you'll get a movie deal next," I said when the server was gone.

"Oh, stop. You're ridiculous. I'm a starving writer at the moment."

I tickled the inside of her palm and said, "You never know."

"What about you? Are you done with this movie?"

I was working on a horror movie releasing the following Halloween. I hated it. I'd never done one before, and I wasn't taking on another.

"Thank God, yes. It's definitely sucking all my creativity. There's no room to do anything different. The cast is great and fun, but I'll be happy when it's over."

"You're such a romantic at heart."

I shook my head, laughing so hard, my eyes were squinting. She was sort of right.

We ate and laughed some more, and then we skipped the tour and went back to my place.

I didn't mind, and neither did she.

Thirty

Charli

We parked in his driveway and my pulse quickened tenfold. I was a wreck. My panties were wet with desire, and my heart was racing on coffee or feelings or both.

It was a cute bungalow tucked back from the street. As soon as I opened my car door, I could hear Harriette barking from inside the house. Layton rolled my suitcase along the concrete, the rattling wheel mimicking the rattle in my lungs.

Lord help me.

"Hey, girl." He opened the front door and a whirl of fur and licks took us over.

"Harriette, meet Charli. Charli, meet the other woman in my life."

"So this is who keeps you warm at night?" It was wishful thinking and prodding all rolled into one on my part.

I didn't want to bring up how much he changed again; I'd already nailed the lid on that issue.

We'd talked about his transformation incessantly over the first few weeks before Layton had finally said, "You changed too, Char. You're doing your own career thing. Less crazed with appearances. You're happier, I believe. So am I. Let it go."

So I did. I'd already spent too many sleepless nights wondering if I didn't deserve Layton because of my past bitchiness.

"Check your fears and all your bullshit at the door," Layton had said, and that's what I was continuing to do, even now.

"She does keep me warm while working, lying at my feet, but there's only one gal in my bed these days, and she's never even seen it."

Oh.

"Come on. Let me get you a glass of water or something and you can relax."

Relax? I wanted him to jump me.

He pointed out the living space and the kitchen, and led me to a small back patio. There I collapsed onto a lounge chair, more tired than I cared to admit.

"Pellegrino?" Layton called from behind the sliding screen door.

"That would be amazing."

He reappeared with a tall glass of bubbly water, a lemon wedge floating at the top, and I took a long sip.

"This is glorious." I sighed, and he sat on the end of the chair and gathered my feet in his lap, slipping my boots off. "That's even better."

"Relax," he told me. "I'm going to walk Harriette around the block so she settles down, and I'll be right back."

All I could do was nod, the sun shining on my face, its heat warming my bones. Or was that Layton?

I didn't know, but I suspected the latter. I felt so good, and within minutes I drifted off.

"Hey, Sleeping Beauty."

I felt his knuckles brush my cheek and my eyes flickered open. "Wow. I didn't mean to do that, fall asleep on you."

"Feel better?"

"Yeah."

He stared at me for a beat, then two, and then he leaned in and brushed his lips against mine. He was perched on the edge of my lounger, next to my hip, and his eyes were wholly focused on me.

"My breath," I murmured into his mouth.

"Is fine," he murmured back before taking advantage of my protest and slipping his tongue inside my mouth.

In one quick move, he leaned over me and released the lounge flat, never moving from my lips. He made sure I didn't fall suddenly, keeping hold of the back of my neck, guiding me slowly into place before he stretched out on top of me.

"This okay?"

When I nodded, he nudged my legs apart with his knee and weaved his legs with mine, pressing his erection into where it counted. My leggings did little to stop the sensation, and I was pretty sure I might orgasm from dry humping in clothes.

Seriously.

His hand moved down my side until his thumb stroked along the waistband of my pants. "I need to touch you a little, mix your scent with mine."

His scent was divine. Piney, a little sweaty and musky from his dog walk. It exuded strength. I would drink it if I could.

The perimeter of the yard was lined with heavy bushes, and tall trees swayed overhead. No one could see us as I arched off the chair, his hand inside my leggings, grazing my most sensitive spot. When I called out his name a moment later, I tried to whisper, not sure if anyone could hear us. But then I didn't care.

With his weight lifted off of me, raised on his elbow, Layton brought me to orgasm right there in his backyard with only a few flicks of his finger. All I could think about was returning the favor.

"Layton," I mumbled.

"Good? Do I make you feel good? Because this makes me feel on top of the world, touching you."

"Yes, oh, yes, Lay."

Rather than pull his hand away, he gave his finger another swirl, a flick, and then a squeeze, and I was riding another wave toward orgasm.

"I want to touch you," I breathed out.

"Right now I'm touching you, beautiful. Later, we'll take care of me."

I wanted to pound his chest and scream *now* but then he slipped two fingers inside me. "Oh God."

My second orgasm hit hard and then I lay like a fish on land. I flopped back on the chair, my back sore from arching and my heart racing to nowhere but getting Layton inside me.

"Can we go inside? Maybe to your room?" I found the moxie to ask in a rather demanding way.

He scooped me up and tossed me over his shoulder, making me gasp with surprised giggles as he slid the screen door open and carried me all the way back to his king-sized bed. He placed me gently on the comforter before shimmying my pants down and gently removing my thong.

Then he took off his jeans, followed by his boxer briefs, gazing at me the entire time. He reached out for my shirt and pulled it over my head. Kneeling, straddling me, he slipped my bra off and traced my nipples with his finger.

I brought my hand under his shirt, wanting to touch him. "Can you take this off?"

"Yeah. It's an old habit."

I scolded myself for forcing the issue but when he removed his shirt, my hands were drawn to his chest like a runner to a finish line. He was handsome, graceful, and hot. His body was made even more beautiful by his insecurity.

He leaned in, still keeping his weight off of me as he reached into his bedside drawer. He set a condom on the bed but ran his erection along me—already dripping and not so eagerly waiting. I lifted my hips to meet him and he slid along my wetness, almost sliding inside me.

Playtime over, he grabbed the condom and wrapped himself, and then he was home. He drove deep, stilling himself at the end of each stroke.

"You're so gorgeous. I could spend forever like this, looking at you," he said when he bottomed out. "But every time I sink inside you is delicious." He moved again, completing the circuit. "And then I pull out, and it's even better when I dip in again."

Layton moaned, I arched, and he picked up speed. We sped to the finish, our skin touching, our scents mixing, and our mouths fused. I came yet again, a record for me, and he didn't last much longer.

He slumped on top of me and ran the tip of his nose over mine. "God, I wanted to wait, but I guess I couldn't. I have no willpower when it comes to us."

Us. That sounded so perfect.

"I'm glad we didn't wait. That was the most fabulous welcome to LA."

He smiled from ear to ear, his eyes sparkling with tiny flecks of amber that glowed in the brown. After he ditched the condom, we spent the rest of the afternoon lazing in his bed. I almost asked if we had to leave, if we could skip meeting his friends.

But I had more willpower than that. Right?

Thirty-One

Layton

Believe me, I'd have much rather stayed buried deep inside Charli, but I'd made plans to meet the guys for happy hour and I couldn't cancel. They were ultra-curious as to who was occupying my free time, even when it was long-distance.

Peter had already texted twice that I'd better be careful or Adam was going to steal my girl. That certainly wasn't helping my desire to go. While she took a shower, I reminded myself Charli liked me before.

I'd given her a fresh towel and left her to do her thing in my room, even though I wanted to join her. I knew if I did, it would be one more reason we didn't make it to happy hour.

I also didn't want to admit my experience in sharing a shower was limited to my senior year of high school and a few semesters of college. Anytime after that, I'd been hesitant to get naked under the bright bathroom lights. The bedroom was one thing but the shower was another.

Which was why I wanted to do it so badly with Charli. It seemed like the universe had good reason for limiting my experience—so the best experiences would be with her.

I heard her shoes click on the floor before I saw her. Harriette let out what seemed to be a murmur of approval, and I looked up. There Charli was in a black sundress that tied around her neck, a pair of strappy Grecian-style sandals and a shimmery silver cardigan hanging from her hand.

"Wow. You look stunning." Her hair was down and blown into straight layers, her eyelids a smoky gray and her lips pink and shiny.

"Thank you. So do you."

I'd quickly showered as she checked her e-mails earlier, and then changed while she was the bathroom. I felt underdressed in my faded jeans and black Coldplay tee. It was from a concert and pretty much a joke. I was trying to replicate the old me in the new me's body, and now I felt like a fool.

"Nah." It was too big and probably looked god-awful.

"I like the tee." She ran her hand down my cheek. "Though I liked him better when he was married. He was lovable as a family man . . . the lead guy."

"I should change. You look like you could be in a magazine, and I'm ready for the neighborhood watering hole."

"Come on." She linked her arm through mine. "I don't want to be late."

We walked toward the ocean, and I held open the door to Bastion's with a knot of regret in my stomach. This wasn't the type of place she was going to like; I just knew it. It wasn't sophisticated or chic.

"Lay!" Peter called from a stool at the bar, and Adam turned around on the stool next to him.

"Hey, guys."

"We're next up at pool, so make the intros quick," Peter said.

Charli laughed.

"Meet Peter and Adam. Guys, meet Charli."

"Hi."

"Girl, you really are all he bragged about. I wish I'd seen a picture. I would've brought my A game tonight."

"Adam," I said through clenched teeth.

"Kidding!"

"You have a good flight and all that?" Peter asked, then sipped at his beer. "Oh, what do you two want? First round is on me."

"Cabernet," Charli quickly replied.

"Beer."

We got our drinks and everything fell into an easier rhythm. Adam and Charli discussed some racy political drama on TV, and then she got on a laughing jag with Peter over some story he told of riding a cab in New York. He claimed the driver drove around the block fifty times, and he let him, wanting to see how far he'd run up the meter. Then Peter got out and did exactly what they said to do. Called the police.

I watched from afar as Charli's chest rose with each laugh and fell with every breath. Her hair swung around her face as she moved, drifting over her shoulder when she gestured with her hands as she talked, and she was at ease.

At some point in the evening, she leaned into my shoulder and said, "I've never had this much fun, never been this happy or relaxed."

I held her close with my hand on her hip, and turned her chin with my finger to kiss her softly. "Good."

We had another drink, a basket of wings (not twelve), veggies and hummus, and a lot more fun. That was the night.

After a few hours and a couple of rounds of pool while Charli watched, I declared, "I'm done sharing my girl."

We said our good-nights, and when Charli kissed my friends on the cheek, I told myself *so the fuck what?* Jealousy raged inside me, but then it was me she held hands with as we left the bar.

Me she leaned into on the walk home.

Me she smiled at.

Me. Me. Me.

I was beginning to become a caveman of epic proportions.

Or a kindergartner who was jealously guarding his toy.

The weekend passed too quickly, which wasn't a big surprise.

On Saturday, after a run and a day at the beach, sitting on a blanket just kissing and whispering, Charli rested her head in my lap, and said, "There's something different out here. I know it's all chic and Hollywood-ish, but it's so natural too. I feel at ease here. There's this organic beauty—and yes, there's smog and honking—but the pace feels so much slower. Better."

I'd wanted to ask her to stay here indefinitely, but I didn't. It was too soon. We'd only just become reacquainted, but we'd been intimate in almost every way. I spent the day warring with myself, wanting to ask her but telling my brain to shut up.

We walked back to my place and tossed the ball to Harriette in the yard as we shared a glass of wine. Passing the pinot grigio back and forth, my mouth over where hers had been and vice versa, I stared at her eyes and saw my heaven.

"I'm falling for you," I said, and she set the goblet on the table and ran her hand up my chest, stopping over my heart.

"I'm falling right back." She rested her forehead next to her hand. "Geez, that's so cliché for a writer, but I am. Falling, and it's so scary. Like one of those dreams where you wake up startled, your breath gone from your lungs, and you feel like you fell down a flight of stairs." Her lips moved against my shirt, her words vibrating against my sternum, each one finding purchase in my heart.

Falling, and it's scary.

I ran my hand down the back of her hair, smoothing the beach-blown waves and keeping her close to me.

"I would never let you get hurt." That's all I said, and then I kissed her. That was enough verbal declarations for one day.

I broke free, whistled for Harriette, and grabbed Charli's hand. We both needed a shower.

I led us to the bathroom and turned on the water before undressing her, shirt first, bra second. I paused for a lick, a nip, and a suck. Her moan filled the room, swirling with the steam pummeling from the shower.

"Want to shower?"

"I thought that was what we were going to do." She ran her hand under my shirt and pulled it off.

We shimmied out of our pants, leaving them and our underwear in a tangled pile on the floor, and stepped under the spray. Warmth enveloped us and I leaned back against the tile, pulling her flush against me, kissing, dancing with her tongue like tomorrow's good-bye was in a minute and this was my last chance.

She slid down my body and dropped to her knees. Her mouth covered me, licking lightly at first and then taking all of me.

As she took me deep and sucked, my head tipped back into the tile. Water continued to rain down on us as she sucked me dry, refusing to move back up until she finished.

"Oh God, Charli, the best," I murmured when she returned to her feet. "Nothing compares to this moment."

Her fingertips traced my arms before grabbing hold of my wrists. "We'll see each other again soon, right? You'll come visit me?"

"Of course."

More kissing, some soaping, and I fell to my knees like a man in love.

Then there was some more kissing of another kind.

Thirty-Two

Charli

Sunday was like a race to touch and kiss and be together as much as we could. We took a short run and came back for Harriette, walking to get some coffee and a muffin to split. Exercise meant something different to Layton. It wasn't about control like it was for me; it was about release. Letting go of the past and being a better person.

It was hard not to get swept up in the emotions and lose myself in the raw beauty of him. Lord knows, I'd been lost in him for two glorious days and I was a goner.

We showered when we got home—not together because we'd probably still be in the shower if we did, and afterward, Layton wanted to show me his studio.

It was the most amazing place I'd ever seen. Wood paneled with soundproof padding on two walls. A huge steel L-shaped desk, tons of audio equipment with lots and lots of buttons. He sat me on his lap and placed a set of headphones over my head.

When he flicked a switch, something hoarse and feely filled my ears. A song for lovers, lyrics that were like tears. Instruments played in the background, but it was the words that captured my attention.

It was a lullaby about warm, sticky nights and twisted sheets and hearts.

Our fingers weave together, gripping palms and fingernails, the sheets twisted around our legs, our souls tangled in one another. I can't ever let go, my heart would shrivel and die, the sheets would evaporate with the world around me . . . the singer crooned.

"That's for my next project. It's an epic love story. The book sold millions of copies and now it's a movie. This is for the scene where they break up. You know, before they get their happy ending."

"It's . . . wow . . . it takes my breath away. Play it again."

He did and we kissed, his hands holding my face tight to his, cupping my cheeks as he made love to my mouth.

And then it was time to go to the airport.

I felt like the sheet was pulled out from under me. My heart shriveled like a prune, just like the song said.

Long kisses and hurried moments—that's how we spent April and May. Layton came to me next and then I went back to him, both of us delaying going to the airport until the last final second.

This long-distance romance was both all-consuming and freeing. I couldn't stop thinking of Layton, yet I'd never felt better about myself. It wasn't only him, although he was the one who got me thinking . . . the man behind my life change. He didn't even know it, but he was.

Seated in 2D, he'd altered the course of my life, pushed over the first domino until all the other tiles fell, and I was writing. Really doing it, and happy. Blissfully at peace.

Except I missed Layton. His scent, touch, and rich laugh were all I was hungry for . . . and ice cream. I was eating it daily, and I didn't care. It was all part of the new me—Charli v. 2.0.

Oh, a small piece of me belonged to Harriette. That dog, she actually made me want to go to California. Her floppy ears, fur everywhere, and sweet eyes (much like her owner), the way she padded around after me, laid at the foot of the bed or the threshold to the bathroom. She was woven into my heart.

Janie was shocked, and I didn't care. My best friend rode it out, accepting all my new nuances. She couldn't help but notice my happiness. I was like a unicorn these days—shooting out rainbows and sparkly stars, that was me.

Me!

In June, Layton and I took a few days off and had a staycation in New York. I locked up my apartment and we checked into Layton's hotel, the one he stayed at when he visited the city.

"Let's paint this place with a better memory than you rushing out on me," he whispered in my ear as we crossed the threshold to a suite.

The air outside was humid and the city quiet while everyone escaped to the Hamptons. We didn't care.

Holed up inside our small bubble, Layton played a playlist from his iPod while we lazed in bed, leaving only to take a run or eat. The restaurants weren't crowded and we lingered at the table, laughing and talking. Mostly staring into each other's eyes and holding hands.

On our last night, we escaped to an Italian bistro and shared a bottle of red and a plate of pasta. Tucked in next to each other in a booth, we didn't even bother with two forks.

"Remember when we had sushi but we didn't share a plate? This is better," Layton said as he pulled me in tight.

He kissed my ear, his breath garlicky from the food and grapey from the wine. I grabbed his cheek and kissed his lips. A closed-mouth kiss, soft and tender, trying to say what I wanted.

Don't go. Stay.

How could I ask that?

I couldn't.

The questions loomed. Where was this going? When would it end? Who would be more brokenhearted?

Me.

I tangled my ankle with his, my small flip-flop resting against his Chuck. I ran my hand down his flat-front shorts to his bare knee, and I got goose bumps. I wanted to run my fingers under the shorts, along his thigh, and up higher, higher.

"This has been magical," I said instead of asking questions.

"It has." His hand rounded my hair, pushing it behind my ear.

"Perfection, one hundred percent."

I pushed a strand of hair away from his eye. He'd let his hair go even longer at my request, and tugging on it had become one of my favorite pastimes.

"Let's get out of here."

He tossed money on the table and we walked back to the hotel, stopping to share an ice cream cone. Lick for lick, we passed the treat back and forth, my tongue running over where his had been.

"Who knew ice cream was so sensual?" I asked, the tip of my tongue lingering on the coolness.

"Oh?"

Layton cocked his eyebrow. Then he stopped on the sidewalk in the middle of Columbus Circle and grabbed the cone for his turn, dabbing it on my lips before licking it off, taking his time with my mouth.

I closed my eyes and imagined a lifetime of this. How did we get there? How did that happen?

It couldn't.

"You're so beautiful, Charleston." He tossed the cone in a garbage and kissed me in earnest. "So damn gorgeous, inside and out," his lips uttered against mine.

I couldn't respond for fear of what kind of crazy proclamations would come spilling out of my mouth. I kissed him back.

"Get a room," a person shouted as they walked by, knocking us out of our tiny world.

"We have one," Layton yelled back, and we laughed as we made our way to the hotel and up in the elevator, falling straight into bed when we got to our room.

He kissed down my neck, biting, sucking, nibbling, and tasting, and I wanted him to feast on me forever.

I love you.

Clothes came off, thrown on the floor, and we were naked, skin to skin, taking and giving. He slid down my body, his tongue taking its time. He lapped my belly-button, ran the tip along where my thigh met my groin, teasing me.

And then he was loving me where I so desperately wanted. My hips reached and he took. Took me there and higher as he brought me to orgasm.

When I wanted to return the favor, he wouldn't let me, pushing his way deep inside my core and riding me to an even higher climax. I had to bite my tongue to keep from waking the entire hotel, and to stop myself from yelling *I love you, forever and ever.*

What the hell were we doing?

Thirty-Three

Charli

*I*n July, I was back to the West Coast for two days, nowhere near enough time, never enough.

What would be enough? How could we measure the adequacy of our time together when we still didn't know what we were? The situation was bordering on lunacy.

We were two broken people, trying to find our way with blinders on because someone was destined to be even more broken when we were done.

One weekend a month, alternating locations, swallowing as much of each other's air as we could in forty-eight to sixty-four hours wasn't even close to enough.

Janie poked fun at our situation, but I knew she was happy for me. We'd worked out and were chatting over coffee one Sunday, both of us stirring our foam into our lattes.

"Janie, I need you to support me in this. I need you because I don't have anyone else," I said matter-of-factly as she took my hand and squeezed our palms together. "I know this wasn't what you wanted for me, but it feels right to me, and you know my mom is so messed up."

"It's probably with both your dad and grandma gone, she's even more focused on you. But I do love you and if this makes you happy, I support you."

She gave my hand another squeeze and leaned over the table and kissed me on the cheek. My affectionate Janie couldn't spend a second without kissing someone.

"Plus, you look so good recently," she said. "If I didn't know better, I'd think you had ass fat injected into your cheeks. You're always smiling and look perkier, and your face doesn't look all sunken in."

"That's the muffins I eat at the coffee shop," I said with a laugh. "Not ass fat."

"Well, you should work for those muffin people because they look good on you."

I shook my head. She was crazy at moments, but the closest thing I had to a sister or confidante.

August turned into a bigger challenge. Layton was working around the clock on three movies and also traveling to Colorado to meet with a smaller studio. I was on deadline for my first book, my editor champing at the bit for my words.

Layton and I met for one glorious night in Arizona. We both flew there Saturday morning and I took the red-eye home on Sunday. Layton took the midnight flight home to Los Angeles. In between, we crawled into bed, ordered room service, and had coffee on our balcony—which was the only time we spent outside the room.

He left a love bite on my thigh and we giggled like teenagers about hickeys.

We watched a bootleg of a movie he worked on, releasing later in the month. He fed me strawberries dipped in champagne in bed. I read him the prologue of my latest work in progress. He made love to me, softly and slowly late Sunday afternoon before we headed to the airport.

I cried on the way home. It was the first time I'd cried. The melancholy surrounding our separating deepened each time I said good-bye. This time, it actually caused physical pain. My chest burned as much as my thighs ached.

But we still hadn't said *I love you.*

There were lots of *I'm falling for you*s and *I miss you*s and *I care so much for you*s. No mentions of love. I knew I did love him, as sure as my tear fell onto the tray of my coach seat.

On my flight home, I reminisced about the first time we met. Layton had been almost invisible to me back then.

Since then, everything had changed. I didn't fly first class anymore. Janie took a step back from managing my love life. I was writing, and eating muffins.

And Layton was now my everything.

The next month, my mom's name popped up on my iPhone as soon as I packed up my stuff at the coffee shop. I thought about screening it, but she'd just call again.

"Hi, Mom."

"Hey, Charli. What's new? Are you still *just* writing?" Her disdain traveled all the way from another state, through the phone and deep into my soul.

"Yes, Mom. I am. That's what I want to do."

It was still sort of nice out, breezy, the sun was beginning to set, so I decided to walk a bit. I connected my earbuds and stuck them in while only half listening to her.

" . . . what happened to your big career?" she was saying. "Graduating early? Dad would've been so proud of all that."

"Mom, I thought that's what I wanted to do, but it wasn't. I'm happy. I wasn't so happy back then. Plus, I'm my own boss now, more responsibility and control."

"You're changing your mind because of the freeloader guy in California."

"Freelancer, not freeloader, Mom."

"Whatever." Deeper disdain filtered through the line.

"Listen, you don't even have to pretend to understand. I have to chase this, and I earned it. I had some savings, which is remarkable in New York, and I haven't even touched the money Dad left me except to put a security deposit on the condo. So, I have to try."

"Well then, you don't have to pretend to understand what I'm about to ask," she countered.

My feet trudged, one in front of the other, my body rigid and wary of what was about to come from her mouth next. Whatever it was, I was certain I wouldn't like it.

"Garrett needs a date this weekend, and you're going. He has some company thing and he really needs someone by his side. It's non-negotiable. I told him yes."

I blew out a long breath and decided to take a run when I got home. Maybe to New Jersey and back? Or however long it took me to burn off my growing tension.

"I can't, Mom. I'm seeing someone."

"He's across the country. Garrett is there and he needs someone. He'll text you later with the details, but it's Saturday, late afternoon, an evening picnic. Period."

"Why are you so set on Garrett?"

"He'll get you back on track."

"I am on track. I don't want to do this." The evening wind cut through my sweater, chilling me to the bone. I started to shiver.

"You will. I'm all alone, a widow, and I asked."

"'Bye, Mom." That was all I could force from my throat before disconnecting.

I knew better than to change the plans. If I did, she'd be on a plane and fixing them to her liking. Whether I liked it or not, I had to do this and get it over with.

Do I tell Layton?

I decided to run to the Pennsylvania border over that thought.

We hadn't been able to figure out a September plan. We were aiming to connect to celebrate our birthdays during the last weekend of the month, hoping to steal four days while my book was at the copy editor and two of his films were wrapped.

I'm not going to lie. I was counting the minutes and it was only midmonth.

I couldn't go through with this Garrett thing. I'd have to find a way out of it, I decided as my feet picked up their pace on the New York streets.

Thirty-Four

Layton

My bare feet were up on the desk in my studio, Harriette on the cool floor, her jowls dripping on the hardwood. We'd just come in from an early evening walk, and I was antsy. Determined to shrug off the feeling, I shoved on my headphones and listened to a few loops of an electric violin solo.

It was perfect.

I let out a loud sigh. I'd been looking for something to pair with an erotic bathroom scene, the last piece of music for this movie, and then I was done. I played the clip on my laptop and matched up the tinny violin strokes with each body movement. The scratchy music fit perfectly with the gruff, tattooed man and the lithe woman onscreen in front of me. He was abrasive like sandpaper and she was smooth like silk. Together, they were explosive and gave new meaning to scratching an itch.

I rewound the clip, made sure the music was set perfectly, and e-mailed it to the producer, confident he would love it.

Leaning back in my chair, I should have felt at ease, but I was even more antsy. All the sexy clips made me miss Charli even more than I already did. I pined for her laughter, the new slight curve of her hips. She hadn't really gained weight; she looked more like a woman filled out in all the right places.

And her smile . . . that smile could light up Manhattan.

I didn't want to share it, though. I wanted all of her grins, each and every one. I would stuff her giggles in my pocket for a rainy day.

Fuck, I'm such a goner. Gone for her.

My mind went to her, to our situation, like it so often did throughout my day.

Although no one had said *I love you*, I wanted to, but I needed it to be right. Charli needed to be settled in her career before I approached her about this. Although her job was sort of transient, but no . . . no, I needed to make a move. I suspected that was pivotal to our relationship working, yet I waited. And now I feared I'd waited too long.

It didn't matter. I missed her so much that my hand twitched, wanting to touch her, to feel her, to slip her hair behind her ear. It was silky like satin sheets fresh from the package.

I should buy some of those, I thought, but then my phone buzzed on my desk.

Adam.

A few guys were grabbing drinks at Bastion's. Looking more closely at the time, I realized it was almost seven on a Friday night. Happy hour was well under way.

I needed to get out of my house for something other than a run or a walk. My mind was playing tricks on me.

She loves me. She loves me not.

Leaving out some fresh water for Harriette, I pulled off my old concert tee and grabbed a Henley. I left my jeans on and slipped into a pair of Reef flip-flops. Why else live at the beach?

Adam clapped me on the shoulder when I bellied up to the bar. "Well, it isn't Romeo! How's it going in lover land?"

"Beer please, whatever's on tap," I said to the bartender.

"That good?" Adam took a sip of his drink.

"It's rough, man. She's not here and I'm not there."

"Star-crossed lovers, that's what I said."

"I heard your little joke, but this is my life."

He lifted his glass to my bottle and said, "Cheers, Lay. Damn straight it's your life. Take control."

"You're kidding. You don't think I have?"

But I hadn't. It was my fault we didn't share our true feelings. I should say it first. I knew she loved me.

"No," Adam said, his tone suddenly sober. "And you know me? No bullshit ever. You took control of your life, even though you almost had it all. Kicking business, lots of pussy, but not her . . ."

"Don't say it," I warned.

"Now you just mope around." Frowning, he said, "Fucking fix it, dude. You want her to move here, ask her. You want to marry her, ask her."

"Whoa, marry? No, we're not there yet."

But the idea did appeal to me . . . a lot. To all of me, my head and my dick. My heart too.

"Drink up and enjoy your night," Adam said as he circled his finger at the bartender for another round. "Wake up tomorrow and do something 'bout this shit."

We drank like he wanted but my mind was elsewhere, concocting a plan. I was going to fucking fix it, all right.

At ten, I left and prayed my neighbor's lights were on. They were, and I knocked softly. Then I grabbed Harriette and delivered her over there before grabbing a duffel and shoving shit inside.

By a quarter to eleven, I was on my way to the airport with one thought in mind.

I was going to fucking fix it.

Physically exhausted, I was running on adrenaline as I made my way to ground transportation at JFK. I needed a cab quickly.

Turned out, I missed the red-eye back east. It left at half past eleven, but the nice old lady working the counter took pity on me and put me at the top of the standby list for the first flight out in the morning. I ended up sitting at the gate for most of the night, too afraid to lose my spot.

By the time I landed in New York, I was wired on caffeine and Charli.

The air was damp when I walked outside, a light mist coating the sidewalk, the sky gray and the leaves in mid-change.

It wasn't the kind of day I'd imagined for us. Back home, I was used to hummingbird-blue skies and hearing the ocean in the background. Maybe that was one of my main issues—I was a California boy at heart. The place had woven itself into my blood, and maybe subconsciously, I worried our love wasn't geographically compatible.

If she wanted me to move here, I would. That's what I decided as I slid into a cab and barked out the name of my regular hotel. I hoped to be surrounded by purple soon enough, but I needed a shower and fresh clothes. Even I knew that spending the night in an airport after drinking beers with buddies and then flying cross-country was no way to meet a woman.

"Crap," I muttered as we hit bumper-to-bumper traffic on the Jersey side of the Lincoln Tunnel. "What's happening?"

"There's parade. Fashion Week."

In September? I closed my eyes, thought hard, and came up short. They paraded around the street for Fashion Week?

"German parade," the cabbie hollered, explaining.

Christ. I leaned back into the dirty seat and took a breath, counted to ten, and exhaled. I did that all the way to Columbus Circle. It took us over an hour.

At the hotel's front desk, I begged for any room as long as it was ready. They took pity on me, which was unusual for New Yorkers. The minute I got to my room, I dialed room service, jumped in the shower, and was out in time for the knock on the door.

With coffee down my throat and toast in my gut, I tossed on jeans, a long-sleeved tee, and Chucks. Fuck it, that was me. She liked the old me.

In the lobby, I paused and texted Charli.

> *Layton: Hey! Happy Saturday! How goes it? I'm just back from a run. You?*

She didn't respond right away, so I decided to take a quick walk. Roaming Central Park South, I was convinced I needed a plan.

By the time I hit Fifth Avenue, my thoughts went haywire.

Finally, she texted back.

> *Charli: Hey, you. Curled on my couch, writing and drinking coffee. I ran on the treadmill this morning. It's raining here.*

No shit. The rain had stopped, but the skies looked like they were about to crack back open.

It should have been a warning.

My conversation with Adam turned in my head, mixing with my love for Santa Monica and my need to have Charli completely. My brain was like a washing machine on the heavy cycle. Thoughts whirred and swished around in one big tangled mess.

The skies parted just as I ducked into a fancy jewelry store and came out twenty-five grand lighter.

I didn't realize how fucked up I was, or that there was more fucking up coming my way. Or that my heart was about to crack in half, like the dark sky above.

I was on a major mission, and nothing was going to stand in my way.

Definitely not New York traffic during a thunderstorm.

I darted into the street and hailed a cab, my free hand in my pocket, fingering my purchase. When a cabbie stopped for me, I jumped into the backseat and rattled off my destination in the Meatpacking District, then closed my eyes, thinking of what I wanted to say.

Water splashed as the tires rolled through puddles, a dull hum of Indian music flitted from the car's radio, and I felt at ease.

I love you.

Thirty-Five

Charli

All the way home, I cursed myself for lying, my hair freshly washed and curled in beach waves that were beginning to droop from the rain. I stood outside my apartment, not wanting to open the door, flipping the key back and forth between my thumb and forefinger.

I just had to get through the next few hours, and then I was going to take charge.

It didn't change how much I despised my mom. There was nothing more to say. She'd thrown down the gauntlet and then shown up out of nowhere, her hair done in some weird seventies Farah Fawcett style, and wearing tight jeans. She resembled the twenty-something version of herself I'd seen in pictures.

Great. She's having some sort of midlife crisis, and my love life is the innocent bystander.

"Hi, Mom," I said, opening my door. She was the one curled up on my couch, listening to rock and roll and drinking coffee. Not me.

"You look great, Charleston. Let's see what you're wearing. He'll be here soon."

"I'm not really up for turning this into a big fashion show. I'm going to get dressed and wait in my bedroom."

Not bothering to remove my wet jacket, I stopped in the kitchen and filled a glass with Pellegrino and stomped back to my bedroom. Of course, my mother had spread out in my living area.

An hour later, I heard the buzzer and my mom yelling into the intercom.

I made my way out in a pair of skinny jeans, knee-high boots, and an eggplant-colored blouse. The event we were going to was a faux picnic, held inside, and only eighty-five percent work-related, like everything in Manhattan. I didn't think the occasion called for flannel, so I opted for business casual.

My mom threw open my door. "Garrett," she said, her voice practically a coo as she greeted him before she called out, "Charli, he's here. Your date." Her voice carried through my small condo.

I felt like saying, *I can see that*, but I wasn't an ornery teenager. Just back to being a bitch.

Garrett stepped inside and smiled at me. "Charli, thanks so much for coming with me."

He was stuffed into one of those tight flannel shirts with the big pockets and rhinestone buttons. He looked so stupid, like a freaking idiot whose secretary dressed him.

"You look great," he told me as my mom smiled at us with approval, sipping a Bloody Mary.

I wanted to roll my eyes. "Thank you. Ready?"

He held out his arm, but I didn't take it.

"'Bye, gang!" my mom called out, so cheerful now that she'd gotten her way.

I didn't bother saying good-bye to her. Honestly, I hoped she was gone when I got back.

"Oh, Charli, come here," she called out before we were out the door. "One sec, Garrett."

Of course, she needed the last word.

"You're taking the pill right?" she whispered into my hair. "Feel free to go back to his place."

"Enough," I replied through clenched teeth.

I met Garrett in the hall and we made our way to the lobby. It seemed to take all his strength to pull open the outer door, and I wondered what he looked like under those clothes. Probably a scrawny little boy-man.

I was cringing to myself when I heard a familiar voice.

"Charli?"

I looked up from the floor. "Layton? What? How?"

I fell over each word, landing on a new question each time. We stood still under the awning, protecting us from the pouring rain but not the impeding shame as we stared at each other.

My "date" shifted at my side. "Excuse me? I'm Garrett."

Oh, now he decides to act like a man?

"I'm Layton."

As Layton looked back and forth between Garrett and me, my throat tightened, clogged with a combination of fear, tears, and screams.

Oh, wait. Those screams were in my head.

"What are you doing here?" I asked.

"I missed you, needed to see you, wanted to surprise you. But I'm thinking now you didn't miss me that much. What the hell?"

I reached out and gripped Layton's bicep, stabilizing myself but also needing to touch him. He was damp from the rain.

"This isn't what you think," I blurted. "I know what it looks like. Please, come in and listen to me. My mom . . ."

Layton shook his head, unable to meet my eyes. "I don't think I can do that right now." He turned away from me and pulled his arm from my grasp, leaving my hand feeling as cold as ice.

"Please," I whimpered.

With all the drama unfolding in front of him, Garrett just stood there staring, not talking or fighting or explaining or defending.

Little boy-man.

"I have to go." Layton ran outside on those words and I followed behind. Luck was on his side—a cab emptied right in front of him and he jumped in, slamming the door behind him.

Devastated, I stood on the sidewalk, tears pouring down my cheeks, cold rain pounding onto my shoulders, unable to move.

"Miss, are you okay?"

Soaked and uncertain how long I'd been standing there, I startled and looked up. Apparently one of the last known friendly New Yorkers had stopped to check on me.

I nodded and murmured, "Yeah," and forced myself out of my stupor.

I looked at my phone. It had been an hour since Garrett showed up at my door to pick me up, and now he was nowhere to be found. My mom was radio silent upstairs in my apartment, and I'd been standing on the sidewalk with the rain dumping on me for close to forty-five minutes.

My feet began to move, and I walked anywhere but home as a tornado whipped up inside my head.

Why didn't Layton listen to me?

Why didn't I chase after him?

Why the hell did I just stand there in the pouring rain?

My boots beat the pavement as rain splashed around my ankles. I remembered my adventures with Layton in the city, our time at the beach in California, and the first moment I laid eyes on him again in February . . . looking so different but his personality just as amazing. He'd been right to run out on me. I was a head case.

My phone buzzed in my pocket, and I looked at who was calling.

"I'm not in the mood, Mom."

"What happened?"

I ducked into a coffee shop, brushed the rain off my jacket, and sat down at a lonely table.

"Mom . . ." My voice was tangled in my vocal cords and tears. "Why did you keep pushing for it? I went and did what you wanted, second-guessed myself, and now I ruined everything before Garrett and I even went to the damn picnic."

"Charleston, you can't keep hauling out to the West Coast for some guy. You'll move out there for him and lose yourself. You're a smart woman, a prodigy, went to college early, started to make a fabulous career. Now you meet this schlepper and turn freelance, and want to go off the grid."

Tears dripped on the table in front of me as I held my forehead in my palm. "Mom, I'm not you, not by a long shot. Was it so bad that you followed Dad on his career? He had goals, and yours were sort of frivolous. Besides, I don't believe he would've stopped you from traveling, seeing things, hearing music. Maybe he would have appreciated going with you sometimes."

"Do you hear yourself? You talk like you know all about love."

"Well, I am in love, but now I've ruined it. Actually, you had a hand in that. Where the hell are you? In my apartment? I want you gone. Seriously." My throat was scratchy and my body as cold as ice. I was dead on the inside.

"Charleston, do you ever wonder why you're named after the city where I met your dad? He was a fling, a guy I met and then decided to tag along with for a while. He was going to Chicago and I'd never been, so I thought why not. Turns out, he'd knocked me up that night we met in Charleston. So, that's you. And that's me. My life after you."

Unable to believe what I was hearing, I swallowed and squeezed my eyes shut.

If I'd thought I was dead moments before, I was six feet under now. Nothing like being twenty-nine when you first find out you weren't wanted.

She thinks I'm a mistake, that I'm the reason why she couldn't do what she wanted.

The waitress didn't ask; she just placed a steaming cup of coffee in front of me and patted me on the shoulder. *Bless her.* I wound my stiff fingers around the mug and let the warmth seep into me.

"Mom, don't. I can't."

"No, you think what I wanted was all frivolous, but it's what I wanted. And then I had a kid who was just like her dad, smart and goal-oriented, and I was forced to play the role of soccer mom. Why? Because my mom told me to. She said *you have a daughter now* . . . blah, blah. When she died, I said screw it. Time for me to be me and you to be you. You want success, six figures, you get a man in New York. I want to hit the road and go to concerts, and the messed-up part of me can't do that until you do what I know you want."

She's crazy.

"Honestly, I don't know what you're going on about," I told her. "It feels disengaged. If you want to be free, you don't have to finish me off like some project."

"Yes, I do, and then I can be free and live with no regrets. Your dad will be happy. He wouldn't want you shacked up with some guy—a music guy, no less, from Cali."

How did I not see any of this coming?

"I have to go, Mom. I can't do this."

I disconnected the call and took a twenty from my clutch. Leaving it on the table, I stood and left.

Not sure whether I could face my mom if she was still at my place, I turned the other direction from home and walked. The rain barely cleansed me from the shame and guilt I felt for giving in to my mom rather than doing what I knew was right.

That was for sure, and I couldn't deny it. No matter how I twisted or turned my words, being a writer wasn't going to help me this time.

Thirty-Six

Layton

Instead of hightailing it back to the airport, I went to my expensive hotel room for one and raided the minibar. After emptying three minibottles of Johnny Walker Black into a tumbler, I knocked half of it back, the burn seizing my throat.

I looked longingly at the chips and nuts, but felt too nauseated to even go there.

Fuck. I paced the length of the room, trying to think straight, tugging my hair until it felt like it was going to come out at the roots.

Who the hell did I think I was in this new body? I was still a fucking joke, that's who.

There was Charli, all put together, perfect for an afternoon out with some equally as perfect dude. Then there was me, sauntering up to the door, a ring burning a gaping hole in my pocket and my heart barreling through my chest with my need to say *I love you.*

I tipped the glass to my lips and tossed back the rest, then slammed the empty tumbler back on the table. Glass shattered and splintered all over my fingers, sending blood trickling out of cuts and fissures.

Like my heart. Except blood was pouring out there.

I shook my hand like an animal as blood dripped on the table, mixing with . . . tears?

Holy shit, was I crying? I was so freaking emotional, as crazy as a teenage girl with PMS, I didn't even register tears dripping down my face.

I went to the bathroom and washed my hand, wrapping it tight in a towel, and went back to the minibar. I shoved a few bottles to the side, sorting through them to find the perfect thing.

Absolut? Nah.

Cognac? Nope.

Tequila? A possibility.

Red wine? That's the ticket.

With my non-injured hand, I picked up the bottle, and of course it reminded me of her. Charli loved her wine. I'd learned over the last few months that a dry cabernet was the way to her heart.

I turned the cap on the tiny bottle, heard the safety seal pop, and took a long whiff. If I tried harder, I could almost smell her breath, cabernet mixed with peppermint. I drained the wine, not even caring anymore what I drank. I just needed to feel numb.

When I dropped on the sofa, something jabbed into my thigh—the ring—and I realized I was nowhere near numb enough. So I got up and snatched the other bottle of red from the minibar and emptied it too, then sulked back into the sofa.

The room spun around me. The painting above the bed looked crooked, and the mirror by the door resembled one of those fat mirrors in a fun house. I leaned back, closed my eyes, and reprimanded my feeble, stupid brain.

Eventually, my eyes dried, my throat clogged, and my breathing was shallow, almost nonexistent. I was a sorry excuse for a man when the phone rang.

I heard it, but didn't see it, a loud shrill in my already aching head. When it stopped and started again, I forced myself up and found the phone next to the bed.

"Hello?"

"Sir, this is Chester at the front desk. I have a young woman here who's demanding to know your room number. Ms. Richards."

Of course she would know where to find me. This was my place, sometimes *our* place when I came to visit. We'd spend a night in a hotel, pretending to be on vacation when all we were doing was borrowing minutes.

Actually, I was stealing them.

"Would you like to speak with her?" the front-desk guy asked.

I'd already forgotten his name, my head was such a clouded, confused mess. "Um, yeah."

A shuffling sounded through the phone before her voice came on the line.

"Lay, listen to me, give me a minute to explain. Let me come up."

Her words were as clogged as mine. I could hear tears in her throat.

"Okay, 1225," I muttered and slammed the receiver down, mistakenly with my cut hand. It started bleeding again.

Shit.

I grabbed another clean towel from the bathroom and held it tight around my fingers. The mess of shattered glass on and around the table caught my eye, and I grabbed a washcloth and swept it all into the trash basket at the end of the table.

There was a soft knock on the door. I glanced around, realizing there was nothing more I could do to cover my fit of rage. I'd ransacked the minibar and the table. Thankfully, there wasn't much else.

When I opened the door, Charli was slumped over, bracing herself on the frame. As she stared at my feet, I did my best to hold my shit together. I told myself to be stoic, impermeable, resistant to her charms. I had to be . . .

And then she looked up. Her eyes were red and swollen, narrow slits, really, and her face smeared in black mascara. She was a mess, and the sight of it devastated me.

I pulled her against me and wrapped my arms around her, holding her tight. She was wet, damp from the rain, her hair a blond bird's nest. I'd never seen her like this—broken—and I couldn't take it.

She sobbed into my chest, and I already hated myself for comforting her. I couldn't control my body; my hand started to stroke her back as I walked us backward into the room and closed the door.

"I'm sorry," she said, sobbing. "It doesn't even cover it; it's not enough. I'm just so, so, so sorry."

Her apology soaked right through my shirt, taking up residence in my heart.

"My mom," she said between hiccups, "told Garrett I'd go to this thing with him, and then showed up here. It doesn't matter, I still agreed to go. But it didn't mean anything."

I hadn't said one word yet, afraid I might spit out something hateful, and at the same time, scared to reveal how broken I was from seeing her with another man. I couldn't be mean, yet I didn't want to be a pushover either.

I leaned against the table in the entrance of my room—I think they call it a crescendo like where our relationship was. A peak, where something was going to happen. Oh no, they called it a credenza. I remembered that's what the nursing home lady said about my parents' room . . . *it has a lovely credenza.*

My mind had gone elsewhere. Somewhere safer. A place where I couldn't hurt anymore.

Charli continued to cry into my chest, mumbling, apologizing. When she grabbed my shoulders and shook me, I realized I wasn't listening.

I closed my eyes and leaned my forehead against hers. "I'm sorry. I zoned out. Honestly, I didn't hear a word you said. I'm not right . . . right now."

She hugged me tight. "I said I was sorry. I know this is my doing, and it was foolish. But it didn't mean anything other than getting my mom off my back. She's been crazy and I couldn't handle it. She doesn't think you're right for me. How could she not?"

Charli dropped to her knees at my dirty Chucks, and it didn't feel right. I wanted her to make her way up to equal footing. This wasn't me. Or her.

"How could she think that?" she cried. "I love you, Layton."

My ears perked up. Afraid I was hearing things, I yanked her to her feet and stared her straight in the eye. "What did you say?"

"I love you." Her eyes welled up again, sending more mascara sliding down her cheeks.

I couldn't stop myself—I kissed her hard.

"That's what I flew here to tell you," I said into her lips, not breaking free. It was messy, her tears mixed with mine, but I kept at it, loving her mouth.

She pulled free and said it again. "I love you."

"I love you too," I said, still fuzzy on what happened with that dude but too relieved to care. Something with her mom . . . Who the hell knew?

"But you kind of stink, Lay."

Tucking her wild hair behind her ear, I admitted, "I had a run-in with the minibar."

"I can smell that." She turned my hand, which was resting gingerly on her hip. "What happened here?"

"I had a run-in with a glass."

"Come on, let me get you cleaned up." She took my good hand and led me to the bathroom, where she turned on the shower.

Her fingers began lifting off my shirt, removing my pants, and it was way too slow. I toed off my shoes and shrugged off my pants, kicked them off my feet. I yanked off her shirt and bent down on the floor, pulling off her boots and sliding her jeans down with one hand. Then I lifted her and pulled us under the warm spray of water.

We kissed long and hard, breaking to lather each other up, our hands touching everywhere we could. She tenderly washed my hand and kissed each one of my knuckles. I ran my good hand down her side, traveling over her side cleavage, my finger sliding over to her nipple and circling it. My fingers got greedy and traveled lower to slide inside her and she moaned out loud, the sound reverberating off the tiles.

I wanted to roar.

I wanted to punch.

I wanted to cry.

But the primal caveman inside me took over, and I savored the woman in front of me. She came on my fingers, bucking and squeezing. I milked it for all it was worth, and then my index finger got bold. It followed the seam of her folds, back to her ass, and toyed with her hole. She clenched her ass cheeks tight and then released them, granting me access.

I'd been down that road before, but not in a glorious ass like this one. Her cheeks were firm, yet ripe. Her hole was tight and puckered, ready and waiting. I traveled past the seam and pushed my way in.

Charli bit my shoulder. "It feels good. Different, but good. Is that weird?"

"It should feel good, and nothing we do should be weird."

Her lips grazed my neck. "Yeah," she said, and she pushed her ass back into my hand.

My erection rubbed against her wet stomach. Our mouths fused again and I greedily swallowed all of her moans as her climax mixed with shower water. When I slid my finger out, she let out a whimper that lit my soul on fire.

"I want you," she said, now riding my thigh. Before I could react, she wrapped her arms around my neck and hoisted herself around my waist.

"Okay?" I wasn't sure why I checked in. She'd gone on the pill two months ago and we'd ditched protection, but after what had happened earlier . . . all of a sudden, I needed reassurance.

"Hey." She kissed my lips, her kiss closed-mouth and full of feeling. "I. Love. You. I've not been with anyone else, even a kiss on the cheek."

The fact she knew what I needed was reassurance enough. I guided myself inside her, going slowly until I was balls-deep.

"Yes," she hissed.

I pressed her back against the tile and tried, really tried, to keep it slow. But I couldn't. Emotion controlled my dick's pace and I rammed into her, holding her steady so her back didn't bruise.

"Yes," she hissed again.

We went at it like that until her release coated me, her beautiful breasts rising and falling with her heavy breaths, and I couldn't last much longer. One pump, two, and I was climaxing. It felt like a dam burst inside me, releasing the misery of the entire afternoon and letting it wash away.

The water turned cool and I shut off the faucet, grabbing two towels from the rack and bundling Charli before wrapping the other around my waist. I hoisted her out of the shower stall and carried her over my shoulder to the bed, where I yanked down the covers and settled her in. I snagged my jeans from our rumpled pile of clothes in the bathroom and checked my pockets before climbing in, grabbing my girl, and never letting go.

With her settled against my chest, I asked, "Smell better?"

Her hand skimmed my stomach. It wasn't quite as toned as when we hooked up in February, but still pretty tight.

"Yes. I'm sorry. This is all my fault."

"Shhh."

Her hand found mine and our fingers entwined. "It is. My mom, I don't even know. She just had this idea and it was all wrong, and I hurt you."

We lay there silently for a beat or two before she asked, "Why are you here? You didn't tell me."

"I missed you and I decided to come. I kept thinking we hadn't said *I love you*, and I wanted to. In person."

A tear trickled down my chest, and then another. Softly, she said, "I wish it didn't play out the way it did."

"You know what? Our story isn't straight and boring, and this just adds a little more flavor."

She squeezed my wrist. "Thanks, but this is more than enough flavor. Bland may be good right about now."

"Nah, like the ice cream you love so much, that's us. Rich, creamy, and it takes a lot of licks to get to the cone. Our cone is strong, babe. A big waffle cone."

"I think you're still drunk."

"Maybe."

"Go to sleep," she whispered, tracing figure-eights on my hand.

"'Kay," was the last thing I remember saying.

Thirty-Seven

Charli

I lay there a long time, awake, somewhat shaken about what path this all could have taken if I didn't find Layton. My mom used to make me laugh with her advice and antics, but she'd gone too far this time.

Why?

And why was Layton so forgiving?

Everything was why, why, why.

My nervous bladder refused to let me rest, and I pried out from underneath him and padded to the bathroom. When I came back out, something by the TV caught my eye. There, halfway underneath the remote and casting a hypnotic prism around the room, sat an engagement ring. I picked it up with shaking fingers and turned it in my hand, hazily remembering him snagging his pants and rummaging through the pockets after he set me in bed.

I guessed he came to say more than *I love you.*

Well, my mom ruined that.

No, I did.

It was time I accepted responsibility for my actions. I went along with Mom's plan, didn't push back. And I'd allowed Janie to bully me when my mom wasn't. I had to accept it all.

"Hey," came from the bed.

Quickly, I set the ring down and turned. I'd been caught.

"I bought that for you."

I stared at the floor, the floral pattern on the rug making faces at me. If I looked hard enough, I could see it sticking its tongue out at me.

Layton stood and walked toward me, pulling me against his chest when he got close. "I'm going to give you a ring, Charli. Just not this one, not today."

"I ruined all this too," I whined, nuzzling my face in his neck.

"You didn't ruin anything. It just wasn't the right time."

His hand ran the length of my back. I was naked, and the warmth of his hand mixed with the cool air caused little goose bumps to raise up all over my skin.

He spoke softly, his breath warming my scalp through my hair. "I really wanted to tell you I didn't want to live apart anymore. I hate the distance between us, and I was thinking I'd move here."

Startled, I glanced up. "What? No, you need to live in LA."

"But you're here."

I shook my head. "I don't want to be."

"Listen, let's go back to bed and discuss this in the morning when we've both had a full night's sleep."

"Okay," I said.

Before I could overthink it, I rejoined him in bed, where he took his time allowing me to fall asleep.

"Mom!" I screamed *loud* enough to wake the whole building. "What the hell are you still doing here?"

She sat up on the couch, blinking owlishly. "You never came back last night, and your phone was off. I was worried."

"Be quiet. No, you weren't, you're just . . ." I waved a hand in the air, exhausted. All the fight had been fucked out of me. "God, I don't even know what. Can you please leave?"

"Where were you?"

"I went to find Layton, who showed up here when I was walking out with Garrett."

"He called me. Garrett, I mean. Not your freeloader," she said, tossing her tangled brown hair over her shoulder.

"You need to go, Mom. Seriously."

"I only want what's best for you. You don't want to be me, fancy-free. Your dad wouldn't have wanted that."

"Please go," I croaked, my throat hoarse and dry. I had no more emotion left in my body. I was dehydrated from feelings.

"Please," she said.

"No." I flashed her the palm of my hand. "Just go."

"Can we talk soon?" She stood, wearing jeans and a rumpled long-sleeved tee, and picked up her duffel at the foot of the couch.

"Maybe soon," was all I could answer.

Thirty-Eight

Layton

"Oh God, holy shit," Charli screamed.

"You sound like you did in bed last night," I said with a smirk.

It felt damn good to be an arrogant hunk for a moment. No way I would let her affection go to my head. She was the kind of girl you spent a lifetime loving and adoring.

I'd come straight to Charli's apartment when I woke up and found her missing.

"Your door was open so I came in, but I'm going to lock it now. This is New York, you know."

Charli scowled at me from her perch on the couch. "My mom slithered out after I begged her to go, and I didn't have the energy to get up."

I kneeled at her feet. "Charleston, about the ring. It was my plan to ask you when I flew here on a whim—"

"Shhh." She ran her hand around my ear, curving my hair behind it. "It's not the time right now. We're figuring things out."

"It's going to happen. You feel that? It's our destiny. Do you want that? Can you love me any way I am? Big or lean?"

She nodded and a single tear dropped onto her cheek. I kissed it away, taking a long inhale of the woman in front of me.

"Lay, I love you and your big heart. That's the only way I see you. The only way I want to see you. This new outside is only a bonus, but the inside is the prize."

I leaned in, wedging myself between her thighs, and tried to kiss her.

"But marriage is so big," she said, "and this whole thing I just went through with my mom . . . God help me, but it seems like her whole marriage to my dad was wrong. So we need to put the ring away. I need to understand why she thinks she made such an epic mistake."

"For now," I mumbled into her mouth and kissed her. "And you may never understand. That's parents. We don't always know why or how or when. Like mine. They were married a long time before they had me. Almost as if one day, they decided, 'Holy shit, we want to be parents.' Then they were too old to even enjoy me and who I became as an adult."

"A wonderful man," she said and her stomach growled, ending our moment.

"Come on. Let's get food, and then we can go see where I can live in this massive city."

"I'm leaving here," Charli declared. "Heading west."

We went out for breakfast and I still refused to believe she was really moving . . . until she wouldn't give up. Girl was stubborn, I'd give her that. She maintained she'd wasted too many years on her career track to be unhappy, and now she was "beyond happy." Her words, not mine.

And she insisted she wanted to be happier where the sun shone and where she could wear "flip-flops instead of stilettos." More of her words.

My girl was a very literal person.

A week later, I received an e-mail from Charli's moving company. Her stuff was arriving in ten days, and she'd be here in eleven. She kept insisting she was going to find her own place, that staying with me was only temporary.

I disagreed, but I didn't tell her that.

Charli was struggling with what happened with her mom, so I didn't push. I knew she wasn't leaving once she moved in with me, though.

Not to mention I had a few tricks up my sleeve. I laughed to myself as I let Harriette outside for a pee break. Oh yeah, I had a few tricks.

I nodded to the construction crew renovating the run-down garage behind my house. I never used the dilapidated thing, but soon it would be a writing studio for Charli. I was putting in new windows, hardwood floors, a kitchenette and bathroom, and painting the whole interior lilac. And she didn't know.

That was only the first part of the plan.

Eleven days later, I went to the airport and grabbed my girl. Charli hurried down the escalator in her flip-flops and jumped into my arms at the bottom.

"Did you ship half of Manhattan to California?"

She laughed into my ear and slid down my body, leaving my chubby on display. "No, only a third. Now are you ready?"

"Oh, I am." I grazed her wrist with my length.

"Come on, let's go."

She grabbed my hand and dragged me out of the airport and back to bed. Before I could show her the garage. Long before Harriette could steal her affections from me (yes, my dog loved her more than me.) Way before I pulled out the other tactics.

That night, we ate sushi on my back patio. Yep, sushi. I'd learned to survive on it at least one night a week. Or maybe I was filled up on Charli? I didn't need a large pie when I had her waiting in my bed for me.

Fuck it, not just my bed but my life. I'd definitely learned moderation since reuniting with the formerly bitchy woman. So had she.

"Do you think it was meant to be? Us, the plane?" She ran her fingers down my forearm while we lay on the lounge chair.

"I don't know. Maybe. I only work in movies."

"I know, but I was on this path to nowhere special, and now I'm here with you, living my life."

"Then it was meant to be." I wrapped our hands together and kissed her earlobe. She was seated between my legs and leaning back on my chest. I breathed in and she breathed out.

"It was. I know it was. You taught me what was important. Oh God, I sound like a sap. But you did."

"I know." I turned her face and kissed her quiet.

I let one week pass before I started pulling rabbits out of my hat. Not rabbits literally, but close enough.

One afternoon as the sun was setting and I knew Charli would be slowing down the banging on her keyboard, I walked across the small yard to her domain.

"Knock, knock." I peeked my head inside the door.

"Hey." She looked up from Lucy v. 2.0. She'd bought herself a new laptop after she signed her book deal.

I took a moment to take in the beauty in front of me. Charli sat at her desk in an old Stones T-shirt of mine. It hung well below the minuscule jean cutoffs she sported. Her bare feet were stretched out in front of her on an exercise ball, and of course, Harriette lay in the corner. The traitorous bitch didn't even raise her head when I walked in.

I was back to wearing music tees most of the time too. I'd gone a tiny bit soft around the middle, mostly due to Charli's love for ice cream and newfound freedom. She was living her life, and I was living mine beside her.

"You finishing?"

She nodded, hit a button, and shut her laptop.

"Come on. We have to be somewhere."

"Really?" She stood and ran her hands down my back, sticking them deep in my back pockets and pulling herself close.

I couldn't help it—I kissed the fuck out of her.

"Yeah, really."

"Should I change?"

"Nah, but I'd put sneakers on. I'll let Harri do her thing while you grab them."

A few minutes later, we were settled in Charli's new car with me driving. She'd bought a convertible, of course. Every transplant to Cali made that mistake. At the moment, she loved riding with the top down, no matter what.

We breezed down the canyon, her long hair flying around her face, her expression relaxed and her smile soft. She was at peace. Way more so than when I met her.

I pulled outside a ranch in the valley. A few kids ran around out front.

Charli gave me a curious look. "What are we doing?"

"You'll see. Come on."

She hesitated getting out of the car, but then I took her hand and led her to the garage.

"Oh. Hey, Layton," the owner of the house called.

"Hey, Mrs. Green! This is my girl, Charli."

"Nice to meet you, Ch—" was all the woman got out before the tiny pup in her arms squirmed free and trotted over the grass.

"Meet your puppy." I pinched Charli's side.

"What? You're nuts. We have Harriette."

"And now we have this little guy. Don't worry, he'll stay little. Maybe twenty pounds."

She picked up the small tri-colored beagle and nuzzled his cheek. Mrs. Green faded into the background but she didn't seem to mind. She'd already been paid.

"He's so cute," Charli said, beaming as she looked up at me. "I'm going to call him Jay after Janie."

"For real?"

"Yes. Her personality is like all this guy's different-colored spots, varied and dark and light. But at the core, she means well."

"I'm not sure she's going to like hearing that you named a dog for her."

"Okay, we'll name him James but call him Jay."

"Deal."

We drove home with the little guy on Charli's lap, stopping for a crate and some food.

That night, curled up in bed with our legs twined together, we kissed and touched.

She rolled over onto her back and sighed. "I'm not going to be able to rent a place that allows me to keep Jay, and soon there'll be no way to separate the two dogs."

"I know," I said, grinning in the darkness. "That was my plan."

Epilogue

Charli

The sun rode high in the sky as I dug my feet in the sand and enjoyed the soothing sound of the water lapping the shore mere feet ahead of me. I breathed deeply, then pulled my hair into a messy bun and slipped my sunglasses on my face.

This was heaven. I didn't know what they were blabbering about when they bitched about the smog here in LA. They'd clearly never tried to get a cab in New York City in a hailstorm, or been shoved into someone's stinky armpit on a crowded subway. Or witnessed what happened to the city after a snowstorm, dirty brown snow piled high by the snowplows.

This was my bliss, this place. Mostly because it was the home of the man who warmed my feet at night.

After a long sip of my decaf iced coffee, I rested my notepad on my lounge chair's built-in tabletop and jotted down some notes. I was working on a love story of the unconventional kind. Girl meets boy and she doesn't really see him; boy meets girl and she's all he can see.

It was our story, I supposed, but I wanted to share it. For all those girls who thought they needed to be this or do that. Sometimes seeing and just being was the key.

My books had zoomed to the top of the *NY Times* bestseller list, and secretly I hoped our story would too. If it did, maybe people who had ever judged someone too quickly would realize it was a terrible sin. And vice versa—maybe those who were all-too-quickly judged would find love at the end of their journey.

It was a Tuesday and the beach was quiet. Seagulls drifted over the water, and the Ferris wheel turned in the distance. A few men and women glistening in sweat ran by, reminding me of my long runs when I first moved here. Layton would always push me to go further, which was sort of funny.

Now I didn't do much more than walking and yoga. For the moment, at least.

My phone dinged at my side, and I rifled through my tote to grab it. I'd only recently given up my place in New York. For a while I sublet it, but it was time to let it go. I wasn't going back. Now I was waiting for the return of my security deposit. I had more important uses for the money these days.

> FROM: LaytonG@darksidemusictracks.com
> TO: Charli@CharliWrites.com
> SUBJECT: Harriette misses you
>
> Hey —
>   Where are you writing today? The beach?
>   Harriette and Jay are lonely and they want to visit you.
> She's begging for the beach, so I'm hoping you have a spot on
> the sand.
>   —Your guy, L

I smiled to myself. *Your guy*. He'd started calling himself that after we made it official, as if there were any competition.

Nope.

Never.

He was my guy since I sat in 2C; I just didn't know it at the time.

I texted him back, not bothering with e-mail, and told him where I was. Even though I was sure he had his suspicions. He'd been on a run when I left home.

The salty air tickled my nose as I went back to my writing. I took a deep breath of it and continued to jot notes, make character sketches, and fill plot holes.

An hour later, Harri poked her nose in my face, licking my chin and nearly bowling me over.

"Hey, girl." I scratched the top of her head and she jutted her chin toward the sky to give me better access, heat radiating off her fur. "Did you get here by yourself?" I moved my scratchy fingers under her jaw and she plopped down at my feet.

A shadow fell over me and I looked up, and there was my guy holding a leash, Jay securely fastened to it. Layton wore a white T-shirt with the Stones logo across his chest, now damp, and loose-fitting Nike shorts. His physique was somewhere between when I met him for the first time and when we came together. He let go more frequently these days, munching fries or cookies, especially considering my current circumstances.

"How's my gang?" He lowered himself to sit next to me, the sand sticking to his sweaty calves.

"We're good."

He brought his lips to mine and rested his hand on my belly, rubbing it in a figure-eight. "Pretty soon it's not going to be just the four of us." A devilish smile spread across his face.

Harriette lifted her head, looking curiously between us as if she knew her life was about to change—yet again.

"So I don't want you to be mad."

I raised my eyebrow over the frame of my sunglasses. "Do tell."

"I thought we should get used to even more chaos, so I got us a puppy."

I tried to stifle a smile. We were having a baby in three months, and Layton decided to do something crazy like this. We'd been living together for a year, so you'd think I'd be used to his enthusiasm, his grand gestures and crazy ideas. Especially when I got pregnant after being in California for six months—Layton was absolutely giddy.

"One of the guys on the set got this pup," he explained, "and there was one more left in the litter. A boy, which was perfect. I thought I'd even the playing field. You know, since there'll be three of you soon."

"Lay, we don't know if it's a girl."

"It is." His eyes, the color of toasted almonds, sparkled in the sunlight, contrasting with the never-ending blue sky behind him.

"You're crazy. Another puppy? I'm definitely paying the price for your quiet childhood."

"I named him Jackie. You've got to see him, all cute and fluffy. And that puppy breath, it's absolutely awful."

"It's a good thing I love you. A puppy? And a baby? We already have Harri and Jay. We must be certifiable."

"I think we kind of need to step up the hunt for a new place."

"You think? Three canines and soon to be three humans?"

Layton averted his eyes, concentrating on Jay. "There's one thing I didn't mention. Jackie is a Newfie, so he's going to get pretty big."

I grabbed the back of Layton's neck, warm from the sun and slick with sweat, and slid my hand through his hair to pull him in for a kiss. It was a better alternative than slapping him.

"So, you're cool with it?"

I kissed him again. His tongue wound its way into my mouth and he deepened the kiss. Of course, my raging hormones took over and I moaned into his lips. My hand roamed his back before slipping into the waistband of his shorts.

"Char, not in my shorts. Not right now." He pulled back a little, a smirk on his face.

"What? I'm horny, fat, and carrying your baby, so it's your job to take care of me. Anyway, when have I never been able to touch you?"

My chest rose and fell, my heart beating a furious pace.

"Oh, I'm going to take care of you. But first, I need to do this." He reached around his back awkwardly, and I realized he was unzipping his pocket.

"Marry me?" he asked, a shiny bauble hanging from his pinky.

"Look at me." I motioned to my belly.

"Yeah? I am looking at you, and I love it."

"I thought we said we weren't going to think about any of that until after the baby."

He raised his hand to my cheek, running his knuckles all the way to the back of my neck. "Are you going to marry me, Charleston? You're not your mom. You're doing what you want. I know we're not in New York but you're doing what you want. Writing by the beach, which is better anyway. I know you think so. Say yes, so I don't get a complex."

"Yes," I whispered into the ocean air. Then I said it louder, afraid it would get lost forever at sea. "Yes!"

"Good," he said and placed a kiss on my closed lips. "I was getting nervous. Luckiest damn day of my life."

"Well, now we have to tell my mom we changed our minds. It will crush her; she was still holding out for a Wall Street banker or something."

Layton chuckled. "She knows I'm your something, she's just afraid to admit it. You know that. She as much as said it, that she felt enormous pressure for you not to turn into a free spirit like her. She wanted you to be like your dad. He grounded her."

"I'm stuck on you being my something," I said while I scribbled it on my notepad. "And I'm totally going to use that line. And yes, my dad centered my mom before I did. Now I don't, and she's pissed. Feels lost."

"As long as you said yes, I'm cool with it. And while you're happy, one more thing. I already called your mom. She knows. I told her I was going to ask you."

Surprised, I asked breathlessly, "What'd she say?"

"She said I better watch my back because Garrett's going to be at the wedding."

We fell into a pile of limbs and laughter on the sand with Harriette jumping all around us, licking every salty surface she could reach, and Jay crawling under us.

Layton

She said yes. That one little word, so small but so significant, ran on repeat in my head. Charli said yes to me!

Later that night, after we went to eat and picked up Jackie from the breeder, we sat on the patio while he nipped at Jay. Harriette ambled over and sniffed the newest addition, and Jackie graciously allowed her to check out all his bits and pieces. When all the dogs lay flat on their stomachs, sick of one another, we went inside.

I smiled to myself as Charli picked up Jackie and nuzzled him into her neck. He was going to be two hundred pounds, and she was loving him like a lap dog. Must have been the nesting thing zapping through her veins.

She walked into our room, slipped him into his crate, and spread a blanket overtop, making it dark and cozy for him before she came to bed. I watched her slip off her sundress, sliding the straps off her shoulders and then letting it flutter to the floor. She wore a white lace bra, barely containing her breasts, and a pair of white booty shorts, her belly protruding over the waistband.

That was our baby. Our girl. Even though we didn't know for certain, I did.

I lay on my back on the bed as I watched, my hands tucked behind my head, Harriette and Jay in the corner.

"Come here."

She kneeled on the bed and I lifted myself up on my elbow, running my free hand over her stomach, exploring every inch, yet unable to take my eyes off my wife-to-be.

"You look so stunning," I told her.

"You have to say that." She pushed me back on the bed, knocking me off my elbow.

"No way. You're gorgeous, and I want you." My voice strained against the lump of desire in my throat.

"Have me," she said, remaining still on her knees.

And I did.

Forever.

the end

Acknowledgments

These damn thank-you's are never-ending for me. I'm wordy when it comes to the people I love and adore.

Thank you, Pam Berehulke, for your editing skills, patience with my need to use crazy punctuation and adverbs, and your steady hand in guiding me away from nine hundred ellipses. Really, just thank you from the bottom of my heart. I *heart* you.

As always, thank you, Sarah Hansen, for loaning me your creative mind. This cover blows me away.

Thank you as always to Emily and Stacey Tippetts for the beautiful formatting and making this book work! And to Tara Jones for the stunning paperback.

For my betas, Robin B., Virginia C., Terilyn S., and Jenn W. Thank you, ladies, for all your kind words, quick turnaround, and pointing out when someone still hasn't taken off their pants so there's no way they could be getting it on yet. :) The life of a romance beta!

Thank you to my family. My husband, sons, mom, aunt, and everyone else who listens to me complain about everything. And I mean *everything*.

To Debra D., the most smiling face on the other end of the computer, for always listening, encouraging, and virtually holding my hand.

To all of my author friends. You're there late at night and early in the morning when the highs and lows of this industry hit. I couldn't ask for more.

Once upon a time, I was a full-time blogger, so I know the hours put into making posts just-so and creating something spectacular. For all the bloggers out there, THANK YOU doesn't really cover it. What you do goes beyond words. There are so many of you who make each and every day better for me.

Huge thanks to Lisa Schilling Hintz, who calms me (often) and makes me laugh. Thanks to her and the entire TRSOR team for the amazing launch, release, and constant shout-outs.

Last, but not least, thank you to Becca Manuel for her fabulous trailers and help at signings, and to Debi Schneider, who impersonates me at signings better than anyone else. Look for her at a signing soon.

Please connect with me in my private reading group, The Electric Readers, where I share insider scoop and casual conversation with my readers.

www.facebook.com/groups/TunnelVIPS/

As well as:

rachelblaufeldauthor@gmail.com
www.rachelblaufeld.com
Twitter @rachelblaufeld

Want to stay in the know?
Sign up for my newsletter. www.rachelblaufeld.com/signup

If you liked this book, feel free to leave a review where you bought it or on Goodreads. Send me an e-mail when you do, and I will thank you personally!

About the Author

Rachel Blaufeld is a social worker/entrepreneur/blogger turned author. Fearless about sharing her opinion, Rachel captured the ear of stay-at-home and working moms on her blog, *BacknGrooveMom*, chronicling her adventures in parenting tweens and inventing a product, often at the same time. She has also blogged for *The Huffington Post*, *Modern Mom*, and *StartupNation*.

Turning her focus on her sometimes wild-and-crazy creative side, it only took Rachel two decades to do exactly what she wanted to do—write a fiction novel. Now she spends way too many hours in local coffee shops plotting her ideas. Her tales may all come with a side of angst and naughtiness, but end lusciously.

Rachel lives around the corner from her childhood home in Pennsylvania with her family and two dogs. Her obsessions include running, coffee, icing-filled doughnuts, antiheroes, and mighty fine epilogues.